The Good, the Bad, and the Pugly
A Little Tombstone Cozy Mystery (Book One)
By Celia Kinsey

Sign up to be notified of Celia's promotions and new releases at **www.celiakinsey.com**

Also by Celia Kinsey

The Little Tombstone Cozy Mysteries
The Good, the Bad, and the Pugly

Lonesome Glove

Tamales at High Noon

Felicia's Food Truck One Hour Mysteries

Chapter One

"Do you have any questions, Mrs. Iverson?" my Great Aunt Geraldine's lawyer asked as I finished reading the first half of my aunt's will and placed it back on his immaculate desk, too overwhelmed to go on.

The surface of the desk was so shiny that I could see that my eyeliner had smudged and that I had a bit of spinach stuck between two of my front teeth.

Aunt Geraldine's lawyer had instructed me to call him Jason, although, as he persisted in addressing me as Mrs. Iverson, rather than Emma, I'd decided it was safer to stick with Mr. Wendell.

"Aunt Geraldine is leaving me Little Tombstone?"

"According to the terms of her will, Mrs. Montgomery has left you nearly everything she possessed, yes," Mr. Wendell said. "The few exceptions are addressed in the later pages."

He smiled an impersonal smile, displaying a row of very white, very straight teeth. I doubted Mr. Wendell ever went around for hours, oblivious to the fact that part of his lunch was on display every time he opened his mouth. At least everyone I'd seen since noon would know I was the sort of responsible citizen who ate her vegetables and did her part to keep rising health care costs at bay by practicing preventative medicine.

I smiled back at Mr. Wendell with my lips pressed firmly together. Smiling with my mouth shut makes me look slightly deranged, but as Mr. Wendell had obviously had extensive dealings with my Great Aunt Geraldine, he shouldn't be surprised to discover that being slightly deranged runs in the family.

"I'm getting the café building?" I asked.

1

"Yes. The Bird Cage Café is included on the deed."

"And the little shop with that funny old man—Hank? He runs that weird museum thingy?"

"The Curio Shop and Museum of the Unexplained, yes. Hank Edwards leases that portion of the premises, although I understand his rent amounts to a purely symbolic sum."

"Hank will become my tenant?"

"In the latter half of the will, Mr. Edward's use of the premises is discussed. It seems your aunt had granted Mr. Edwards tenancy for life at what seemed to me a rather reduced rent."

"How reduced?"

"The will stipulates the rent to remain, in perpetuity, at ten dollars a month."

If I hadn't been so shocked by the will in its entirety, I would have asked a lot more questions about the relationship between Hank Edwards and my Great Aunt Geraldine—not that Mr. Wendell would have been in a position to answer them—but I didn't. At the moment, I had more pressing concerns.

"Aunt Geraldine left me the trailer court too?"

"Yes, also with several long-term tenants, although I won't deceive you that the rents amount to much. You are free to raise those rents, unlike Mr. Edwards', at your discretion."

"And the motel?"

"There are the two tourist cottages as well as the eight-room motel, all of which are vacant and virtually derelict."

"If Aunt Geraldine was this loaded," I pointed down at the documents on Mr. Wendell's desk, "why is Little Tombstone in such bad shape?"

"I'm afraid Mrs. Montgomery did not confide in me her reasons for allowing things to run into such disrepair."

"But what about Abigail?" I asked. "Shouldn't she be the one getting all this?"

"Mrs. Montgomery's daughter?"

My cousin Abigail had been on the outs with her mother off and on for years, but I had a hard time believing that their relationship had deteriorated to the extent that my Aunt Geraldine would cut her daughter out of the will entirely.

"Mrs. Montgomery did leave her daughter a small bequest," Mr. Wendell said. "You'll find it on page eighteen."

I consulted page eighteen.

"'A blue 1978 Oldsmobile Cutlass Supreme with an extra set of hubcaps (needs new carburetor and windshield, hood ornament missing).' What about Abigail's daughters?"

"Keep reading," said Mr. Wendell. "Mrs. Montgomery left something for each of her granddaughters."

I scanned the page once more.

"A large box of miscellaneous Tupperware (some have lids) for Freida and a set of World Book Encyclopedias (missing volume B and U-V) for Georgia?" I said. "Isn't this all a bit insulting?"

"It's not my place to interpret the intent of the deceased," said Mr. Wendell, and for a few seconds his stuffed-frog demeanor slipped a little, "but I have reason to believe that Mrs. Montgomery may have been less than pleased with her daughter and granddaughters at the time of her death. Mrs. Montgomery altered the will, shortly before she died, to leave her real estate and the bulk of her personal property to you. Your name was added as sole beneficiary to all her banking and investment accounts at the same time Mrs. Montgomery altered her will. Those accounts are not reflected in the will itself, and their existence may be kept confidential if you wish."

3

"But why would my Great Aunt Geraldine leave me practically everything?"

"I believe that your grandmother had specified that her half of Little Tombstone should pass on to you upon your aunt's death. I understand that it was joint property between your great aunt and your grandmother. The earlier version of the will had named you and your cousin Abigail as joint inheritors of Little Tombstone, but your great aunt must have had misgivings about the arrangement."

I checked the date on the will. It had been signed just three weeks before Great Aunt Geraldine had passed away.

"But I didn't even come to see Aunt Geraldine when she was sick," I said. "I haven't visited Little Tombstone for almost three years. I always called my aunt at Christmas and on her birthday, but that's about it. I don't deserve this."

The truth was, I hadn't known my great aunt even had cancer until I'd received a call from Aunt Geraldine's best friend, Juanita, telling me that my aunt was already gone. There'd been no service, just a quiet cremation.

I'd inherited Great Aunt Geraldine's ashes too, apparently. The bright blue ceramic urn containing all that was left of my aunt sat on Mr. Wendell's shiny desk next to the manila envelope which held my copy of the will.

"Your aunt did not confide in me her reasons for leaving you the bulk of her property. The only comment she made when she came in to draft the changes was that she was doing it for Earp."

"Earp? Aunt Geraldine's dog, you mean?"

I was shocked that Earp was still alive. I'd not been back to visit Little Tombstone since my grandmother's funeral three years before, and even then, Earp, my Great Aunt Geraldine's ancient

4

and irritable pug, had looked about a hundred years old—in dog years, of course.

Earp had taken an obsessive shine to me. I suspected that it was not my personal charm that fueled his possessiveness, but because I surreptitiously fed him little powdered sugar-covered lemon cookies out of the package I always keep in my handbag. Whatever the reason, for my entire visit to Little Tombstone, Earp had refused to let me out of his sight.

"You've not made it to the section addressing the matter of Earp," said Mr. Wendell. His lip twitched a bit at one corner as if suppressing a genuine smile of amusement, but he hastily replaced it with a professional display of his straight, white teeth. "If you'll skip to page nine, you'll find the matter of Earp addressed in great detail."

I read page nine, then page ten, followed by pages eleven through thirteen. By the time I was finished reading the lengthy passages addressing the care, feeding, and sweatering of the pug, I understood why Mr. Stiff-as-a-Double-Starched-Shirt was having trouble keeping a straight face.

There was a condition attached to my inheritance of Little Tombstone Café, Curios, Museum, and Trailer Court: I was obliged to Love, Honor, and Cherish my Aunt Geraldine's beloved pug 'til death-do-us-part. Those were her exact words.

If I didn't, Little Tombstone, along with what appeared to be a substantial stash of cash and even more substantial investments, would go to the Animal Rescue in Albuquerque, and all I'd be left with was an old set of golf clubs formerly used by my late Uncle Ricky to hit rocks at rattlesnakes.

Chapter Two

After I had finished reading the will and asked at least a million questions, all of which Mr. Wendell patiently answered, he insisted on accompanying me to Little Tombstone.

"Just in case," he said.

"Just in case of what?" I asked, but Mr. Wendell ignored my question and instructed me to follow his spotless, white, and nearly-new Land Rover in my compact rental car.

I wondered what someone who drove a spotless, white, and nearly-new Land Rover and wore what looked suspiciously like handmade Italian leather loafers was doing practicing law in a dusty New Mexican wide-spot in the road. Even Mr. Wendell's small concrete office building looked out of place. It was the newest structure of the twenty-odd buildings that made up the village of Amatista by a good thirty years.

Mr. Wendell looked more like the Santa Fe type. I'd have thought he'd be well suited to intellectual property law or corporate mediation, rather than officiating the wills of eccentrics who bequeath rundown roadside tourist attractions to their down-and-out grandnieces.

I wondered if Mr. Wendell handled divorces. I'd already filed for one in LA County, but after seeing what Aunt Geraldine was apparently leaving me, I was in no mood to let my fiscally reckless ex get his hands on that, too.

I'd selected my LA lawyer by the dubious strategy of performing an internet search for divorce attorneys and then picking one at random. It was all I'd had strength for at the time.

It might do to get a second opinion, just in case my first arbitrary pick of legal counsel was giving me bad advice.

When we reached Little Tombstone, a mere half-mile north of Mr. Wendell's office, it looked much as I had left it three years before. Little Tombstone had looked shabby then, and it looked shabby now.

According to the deed, which I'd received along with Aunt Geraldine's will, Little Tombstone sat on one hundred and fifty acres, but the buildings were clustered on three blocks' worth of street frontage along Highway 14. The buildings were on the far north edge of the tiny village of Amatista, but the bulk of the land attached to Little Tombstone extended into rolling hills dotted with sagebrush and cactus interrupted by the occasional arroyo.

Little Tombstone proper—a haphazard and truncated imitation of the original historic town in Arizona—had originally been my grandfather's idea, back in the 1970s, but his idea had outlived him by forty years. After my grandfather's unexpected death left my grandmother a very young and overwhelmed single mother raising a daughter on her own, she had invited her sister Geraldine and Geraldine's husband, Ricky, to move to Amatista and help run the roadside attraction—then in its heyday.

Judging by the condition of the place, Little Tombstone's heyday was over, never to return.

Mr. Wendell bypassed the eight-unit motel with its broken-out windows and collapsing roof and pulled up in front of the Bird Cage Café, the only building within the three blocks' worth of weather-beaten structures which had any cars parked in front of it. I pulled into the gravel strip which fronted the dilapidated boardwalk that tied the whole crumbling monstrosity together.

Mr. Wendell climbed out of his Land Rover and navigated the broken steps leading up to the elevated boardwalk with a look on his face that plainly said, "This place is a personal injury lawsuit waiting to happen."

I made a mental note to use a bit of the cash my Great Aunt Geraldine had left sitting in the bank to get someone out to fix those steps before some poor soul broke his neck.

I'd always assumed that Aunt Geraldine had let things get in such a sorry state because she lacked the funds to do anything about it, but, based on the assets enumerated in the list, I'd just received from my aunt's lawyer, I'd assumed wrong. Aunt Geraldine had been practically rolling in dough.

Mr. Wendell held open the swinging saloon-style doors which led into a small open-air vestibule.

"You may find that Mrs. Gonzales is still somewhat distraught over your great aunt's passing," he said as we paused in front of the glass door which led into the café's dining room.

I noticed one of the panes of glass in the door was broken out and had been covered over with an old license plate screwed haphazardly to the frame.

As Mr. Wendell pushed open the door, a bell jingled overhead. The dining room was empty except for a wizened old man I immediately recognized as Hank, the proprietor of the Curio Shop and curator of the Museum of the Unexplained next door.

Hank was sitting at a table for two in the back corner sipping a cup of coffee and smoking a cigar. He'd overturned one of the little plastic No Smoking signs that sat on each table and was using it as an improvised ashtray.

"Morning, Mr. Edwards," said Mr. Wendell.

Hank just grunted and took another draw on his cigar.

"You remember Mrs. Iverson."

Hank grunted again, allowing his gaze to hover somewhere east of my left ear. Hank looked none too happy to see me, although, if my memory served me correctly, none too happy was Hank Edwards' perpetual state of mind.

I could hear Juanita in the back, banging pots and singing at the top of her lungs. She didn't sound terribly devastated, but then she was the type who could laugh through her tears, so I concluded that Mr. Wendell's read on the situation was probably accurate.

Juanita had almost forty years of friendship with my Aunt Geraldine to look back on. Nobody gets over a loss like that overnight.

Mr. Wendell and I left Hank to his coffee and his probably-not-legal-on-the-premises-of-a-food-service-establishment-open-to-the-public-in-the-state-of-New-Mexico cigar and went through to the kitchen.

As soon as Juanita clapped eyes on me, she proceeded to maul me in a motherly fashion which I've always found incredibly endearing. Both my grandmother and my great aunt had been raised up under the "a handshake is as good as a hug" school of thought, and they'd instilled the same philosophy in my late mother. During my childhood, hugs had been in short supply. Still, every time I'd been to visit Little Tombstone, Juanita had more than made up for my flesh and blood's standoffishness by practically squeezing the stuffing out of me every chance she got.

"Emma!" she said, "You've—"

I half expected Juanita to tell me I'd grown. It was true. I had grown. Outward. Which is the only way that thirty-three-year-olds generally do grow. I had gained fifteen pounds in the last three months. Stress-eating will do that to a person.

I guess Juanita realized that it would be insensitive to point out my weight gain, so she finished with, "—changed your hair."

I hadn't, not since she'd last seen me, but I wasn't about to argue with her in front of Mr. Wendell.

"You've seen Hank?" she asked.

"Yes, he—umm—greeted us as we came through," I said.

I wondered when Mr. Wendell was going to leave. It appeared he planned to conduct me on a complete tour of Little Tombstone, a place I'd been coming to all my life. I hoped he wasn't billing me by the hour for his services.

"You can go," I told him. "Thanks for bringing me out here, but I'll be fine on my own now."

For the first time since I'd met him, Mr. Wendell appeared flustered.

"Have you had lunch?" Juanita asked. It was nearly four in the afternoon. I'd had lunch hours ago. Skipping meals is not something I do if I can help it. Truthfully, the soggy chicken sandwich and anemic spinach salad I'd eaten at the Albuquerque airport before picking up my rental car had worn off sometime halfway through the reading of my Great Aunt Geraldine's will.

"I could eat," I said.

The Bird Cage Café might not look like much. It might have broken down steps and a broken down clientele who haunted it, but it had Juanita Gonzales, and Juanita Gonzales made the best food I'd ever eaten. I'd been eating Juanita's food for as long as I'd been old enough to lift a fork, and I'd yet to come across anyone who could rival her.

"What about you, Jason?" Juanita asked. "Could you manage a bite?"

Mr. Wendell nodded. I wondered if he was a regular at the Bird Cage Café. He didn't look like the sort who'd patronize such a rough-around-the-edges establishment, but maybe there was more to him than his handmade Italian leather loafers implied.

"I made fresh tamales this morning," said Juanita, without giving us an opportunity to order. "I'll bring you both a plate."

I sat down at the table farthest from Hank, who was still working on his cigar and pretending he was the only one in the room.

Mr. Wendell walked to the front of the dining room and cracked open a window before coming and sitting down across from me. I hoped he wasn't planning to charge me 200 dollars an hour to watch him eat Juanita's tamales.

While we were waiting for Juanita to return with our plates, the front door opened, and a generically pretty blonde of about twenty came in. She was wearing an apron over a ruffled dress that looked utterly unequal to the task of holding up to grease and green sauce. I wondered where Juanita had found her.

The waitress beamed in our direction—well, mostly in Mr. Wendell's direction—before disappearing into the kitchen. She didn't even look over at Hank. Apparently, Hank was such a fixture he didn't bear acknowledgment.

"Who's that?" I asked Mr. Wendell.

"Chamomile."

"Like the tea?"

Mr. Wendell nodded. "Chamomile is Katie's daughter."

"Who's Katie?"

"One of your tenants at the trailer court."

I wracked my brain. I didn't recall any Katie. The last time I'd visited Little Tombstone, there'd been only two permanent

12

residents of the trailer court, although there'd be the odd vacationer or snowbird who'd take one of the empty slots from time to time.

As I recalled, there were only two tenants: Morticia the Psychic—I never had asked about her real name—perhaps her parents had been diehard fans of The Adams Family, and Morticia **was** her real name—and Marcus Ledbetter, who went by his last name. Ledbetter was a veteran of the war in Afghanistan. My aunt Geraldine had once explained that Ledbetter suffered from PTSD, and that was why he rarely left his trailer.

"Katie must be a new tenant," I said.

"I moved here two years ago," Mr. Wendell told me, "and she was living here then. Katie's the mail carrier for Amatista. She does the rural route."

I was about to make a smart remark about the rural route being the only route Amatista had, but then I remembered that everyone within village limits had to collect their mail directly from the post office and realized that I'd just be stating the obvious. Besides, Mr. Wendell had the air of a man with a severely limited capacity for sarcasm.

Juanita emerged from the kitchen carrying two steaming plates of tamales. Chamomile brought up the rear with two tall glasses of iced tea.

After patting me affectionately on the cheek, Juanita withdrew to the kitchen.

Before following her, Chamomile bestowed an unnecessarily sunny smile on Mr. Wendell. She even tossed her flaxen hair a little and batted her fake lashes, something I'd never seen anyone do in real life. Clearly, Chamomile had a thing for the man, but Mr. Wendell appeared immune to her charms.

13

It struck me as odd that Chamomile would be interested in Mr. Wendell, considering he must be closing in on thirty, but after I thought about it for a few seconds more, it no longer seemed so strange. Mr. Wendell might be one of only a handful of men in the village of Amatista who was both gainfully employed and still had all his own teeth. Mr. Wendell was undoubtedly the only man who drove a spotless Land Rover and wore custom-made shoes. He wasn't bad looking, either, provided one could get past the starchiness.

Just in case I was paying for the privilege of dining with Amatista's most eligible bachelor—

if the absence of a ring on Mr. Wendell's left hand could be believed—I decided to pump him for legal advice.

"I'm getting a divorce," I said.

Mr. Wendell practically jumped. His fork clattered to his plate, spattering his spotless white shirtfront with salsa verde.

"Pardon?" he said.

"I'm getting a divorce," I repeated. "I mean, you being a lawyer and all, I thought I might ask you a few questions since you're right here in front of me unless this is strictly off-the-clock."

"No, no, ask away," Mr. Wendell said, leaving me more in the dark than ever as to whether he considered eating tamales with me as part of his duties as executor of my great aunt's estate or if he was planning to present me with a bill later on for legal services rendered while eating Mexican food.

"It's about the will," I said. "Could my soon-to-be-ex-husband claim a portion of what Aunt Geraldine left me?"

"You've already filed for divorce?"

"Yes."

"In the state of California?"

14

"Yes."

"Property acquired by gift or inheritance during the marriage is that spouse's separate property. Additionally, many states—and I believe that California is one of them—also provide that property spouses acquire before the divorce but after the date of legal separation is separate property." He managed to sound as if he were reading off a legal document, even though there was nothing in front of him.

"Good to know," I said. "Can I ask you something else?"

Mr. Wendell was distracted. He'd noticed the sullied purity of his shirt front and was futilely dabbing at the green speckles on his chest with a paper napkin.

"Hydrogen peroxide," I suggested.

"What?"

"For the stain. Full strength hydrogen peroxide before you put it in the washer. I'm an expert on stains. I'm always spilling something on myself."

Mr. Wendell looked up at me as if to say he'd thought as much, even though I hadn't managed to get anything on myself. Yet.

"What's your other question?" he asked.

"How would I go about recovering an investment I'd made in my husband's business?"

"Do you have any legal interest in the business?"

"No. My husband is a cosmetic surgeon."

Mr. Wendell looked surprised. I don't look like the wife of a cosmetic surgeon. Frank—my husband—was always offering helpful little hints on how I could improve myself—or rather how he could improve me—but I never took him up on any of his offers, not even for a bit of Botox.

15

"If you could provide me with supporting documentation and specific details, I could better advise you."

"He doesn't have it anymore," I told Mr. Wendell.

"The cosmetic surgery practice?"

"No, the money." I was babbling now. I'd been up since three a.m., Pacific Time, and the shock of finding out that Great Aunt Geraldine had left me all her earthly goods, plus Earp, was contributing to my feeling that this was all just a weird dream.

"Your husband took off with the money?"

"No, Shirley did."

"Who's Shirley?"

"His business manager." And his mistress, but I didn't feel like telling Mr. Wendell that. Shirley was the reason Frank and I were getting a divorce, and it wasn't just because Shirley had stolen every last cent of what I'd earned from finally selling my screenplay. That money was supposed to be paying for Frank's big office remodel, and Shirley had gone and blown it at the roulette tables in Vegas.

I might have carried on and told Mr. Wendell the whole torrid tale, except that we were interrupted by Hank.

"You're the new landlady," Hank said. It was a statement of fact, not a question.

"That's what he tells me," I said, pointing across the table at Mr. Wendell.

"Well, I want to know what you're going to do about our little problem," Hank said.

"I'll get to work right away on getting stuff repaired," I said. "I'm sure there are hundreds of things that need fixing, so I'll need to prioritize. If you could make me a list of the most urgent—"

"I don't mean that," said Hank. "I want to know what you're going to do about our alien invaders!"

Chapter Three

"I suppose there's no chance that was Hank's offensive way of demanding that I evict a family of undocumented immigrants, is there?" I asked Mr. Wendell after Hank had left the café, taking his cigar with him.

"When Mr. Edwards refers to aliens," Mr. Wendell said, "I'm afraid he's speaking of extraterrestrials."

"Is that Hank's new thing? Aliens? Last I knew he was obsessed with inventing an engine that would run on water, not little green people."

"You'll have to ask someone else about Mr. Edwards' current areas of interest," said Mr. Wendell, pushing back his chair and standing to his feet. "Now, before I go, I feel it is my duty to confirm that Earp consents to your aunt's arrangements for his future."

We'd finished our tamales, and Juanita emerged from the kitchen to inform us that our meal was on the house.

"I'll come back and see you," I told her, "once I've seen Earp."

"Morticia will be overjoyed to have you take Earp off her hands," Juanita said. "The little rascal doesn't seem to like Morticia very much, but she's who your Aunt Geraldine named as his guardian until you could take over."

The trailer court occupied a tumbleweed-strewn lot behind the derelict motel. One corner was taken up by a couple of run-down tourist cottages, and the remainder by a double row of narrow concrete slabs with a gravel alley running down the middle. Only three of the twelve slots were occupied.

Morticia's motorhome, which functioned both as her home and business premises, was easily the most striking feature of the trailer court. It occupied the prime position nearest the side street.

There was no danger of anyone passing by without noticing Morticia's ancient Winnebago. She'd painted it every color of the rainbow, and the central feature of the design was an enormous, vaguely menacing eye painted on the side. Underneath the eye were the words: Tarot. Your Future Foretold. Free 10-Minute Readings.

Morticia never charged for the first ten minutes, but she'd always make some break-through discovery at the nine-and-a-half-minute mark. Surprisingly often, according to my Aunt Geraldine, Morticia's hapless clients would happily fork over her standard rate of three dollars a minute to hear what the cards had belatedly revealed.

Morticia answered the door on my first knock. The smell of incense wafted out the open door of the Winnebago, and from within the patchouli-scented interior, I heard a miniature sneeze.

"Sorry about your aunt," Morticia said without preamble. "Somebody should have told you she was sick. I'd have called you myself if I'd known Geraldine was keeping it from you."

"That's all right," I said.

Me knowing she'd had cancer wouldn't have prevented my Great Aunt Geraldine from dying. Even though part of me was mad at her for going and dying like that without even giving me a chance to say goodbye, part of me understood. Aunt Geraldine had always had her own unique way of doing things, and who was I to say how she should have handled the realization that she was going to die?

"Earp in there?" I asked. "Was that him that sneezed?"

"Yeah," Morticia said. "He hates the incense, but it's essential to creating the proper atmosphere, so I make him put up with it."

"Earp," I called out.

I heard the dull thud of a small body hitting the floor, and two seconds later, my shins were being pelted by an elderly pug who seemed unreasonably excited to see me. Earp wasn't the dog he used to be, but considering his advanced age, he was still remarkably springy. Every time he jumped, Earp got his nose an inch closer to my handbag.

"Cookies," I told Morticia.

"Cookies?"

"Gingersnaps, to be exact," I said, withdrawing a small cookie from my handbag and feeding it to Earp.

Now that I was responsible for Earp's health and well-being, I'd have to start carrying something better for an elderly dog than gingersnaps, but just this once for old time's sake, I was prepared to indulge him.

I noticed that Earp, unlike when his mistress had been alive, was going around in the nude. I wondered what had become of Aunt Geraldine's extensive collection of doggy costumes and festive sweaters. I was guessing that, much as Earp might miss my aunt, he wasn't missing the indignity of getting shoved into some ridiculous outfit every morning.

It was only three weeks until Thanksgiving. Had my great aunt still been with us, Earp would have been dressed, on alternate days, either as a tiny stove-pipe-hatted pilgrim father or a turkey, complete with tail feathers.

The cookie seemed to calm Earp down a bit, so I reached down and picked him up. He settled into my arms and sighed.

"How do you manage that?" Morticia said. "If I try to pick him up, he growls at me."

I shrugged. It was a mystery to me, too.

"I'll be going," said Mr. Wendell, who'd been standing off to the side while Earp and I were reunited.

"You want a reading before you go?" Morticia asked him, glancing speculatively at his custom-made shoes and $200 haircut. "First ten minutes are free."

And the subsequent minutes would be calculated to come out to whatever amount Morticia suspected Mr. Wendell carried on him in cash. I was guessing about $500 in a mixture of hundreds and fifties, although Morticia would really be forced to exercise her creativity to get a reading to go on that long at a rate of three dollars a minute.

"Go on," I told Mr. Wendell. "If you go over ten minutes, it's on me. I've been recently informed that my days of financial insolvency are suddenly over."

Earp had snuggled down and tucked his nose under the floppy sleeve of my sweater. He was emitting contented snores at regular intervals.

"I don't think—" Mr. Wendell protested.

"I think it's the responsibility of us all to support local businesses whenever possible," I said.

Mr. Wendell hesitated, which was all the permission Morticia needed to clutch the sleeve of his crisp white shirt between her crimson-painted fingernails and tug him up the steps into her motorhome.

I thought Morticia was going to succeed, and I would have considered it money well spent to see a man like Mr. Wendell sit through one of Morticia's readings, but it was not to be.

22

I'd followed them inside, and as I navigated the dark and cramped interior of Morticia's motorhome, I stubbed my toe.

"Ouch!"

My outcry startled Earp out of dreamland. He yelped and pawed at my sweater until I set him down on the floor. Still agitated, he shot out the open door of Morticia's Winnebago and took off at a pace I would not have thought possible for a dog of his advanced years.

I gave chase, but every time I'd get close enough to try and lure him back with a ginger snap he'd remain just out of my reach. I tossed a ginger snap to Earp in hopes of getting him to come closer for a second cookie, but instead of coming closer he took the ginger snap in his teeth, retreated under Ledbetter's trailer, and started to dig.

At first, I thought he intended to bury the cookie for consumption later on, but it soon became apparent that Earp had already eaten the cookie and was digging something up, rather than burying it. Ledbetter's trailer was parked in one of the two slots in the trailer court which didn't have a concrete pad underneath, and Earp created quite a cloud of dust with his vigorous efforts.

I got down on my belly to watch him work. He clearly was not going to come out until he'd completed his job. Morticia sat on the steps of her motorhome, transparently amused and relieved that Earp was no longer her problem. Mr. Wendell stood just far enough off to avoid getting any flying dust on his luxurious loafers.

Earp dug for fifteen minutes, gradually unearthing his treasure. He emerged from under the trailer, and I awkwardly got up off my stomach and started to brush about three pounds of dirt off the front of my sweater in preparation for giving chase again, but pursuit was not necessary. Earp trotted right up to me and dropped his treasure at my feet.

"Is this a present?" I asked him. He gave a little bark and flopped down on the ground next to the gift, exhausted from the exertion of moving six times his body weight in dirt and gravel.

I picked up my present. It was the weathered leg bone of a fairly large animal, obviously an old favorite of Earp's because one end had been chewed almost to splinters.

"Do you think this is a cow bone?" I asked Mr. Wendell. "It looks too big to belong to a deer."

"I don't think that's from a cow," Mr. Wendell said, taking the bone from me and examining it. "I can't say for sure, but it looks suspiciously like a human femur."

Chapter Four

"It probably is a human bone," said Morticia, making me jump nearly out of my skin. She'd come up soundlessly behind us. "The first time Earp dragged one of those things in, it creeped me out," she continued, "but then I asked around and found out that a couple of the graves from the old cemetery up on the hill have suffered from erosion, so I figured—"

Mr. Wendell offered the bone back to me, but I declined.

"That's disgusting," I said. "And disrespectful to the dead. Why doesn't anybody do anything about it?"

"Oh, I told your Aunt Geraldine, and she called the county. They sent a couple of guys from the road crew out to the cemetery with shovels," Morticia said, "but I don't think a man with a shovel is going to do much good against half a hillside slowly washing away. Those graves need to be dug up and moved, but they are so old that the families of the deceased are long gone, too, so who's going to foot the bill for moving them somewhere else?"

"What do we do with this bone?" I asked.

"There's a banana box half full of bones in room two of the old motel. I decided to put them there for safekeeping. That way, if anybody ever does dig up those graves and tries to put the pieces back together, at least they'll have something to work with. At the rate Earp is dragging in bones, though, we'll soon collect enough to assemble a whole skeleton."

After Mr. Wendell went back to his office, I went back to the café to talk to Juanita. It was close to six by this time, and the place was filling up.

"I'll come back later," I told her, "after the supper rush is over. Is Chamomile all the help you've got around here?"

"No," Juanita glanced around and lowered her voice. "I've got Marco in the dish room. I hired him to bus tables because he's Pastor Freddy's son."

Juanita is a big churchgoer. There are two tiny religious congregations in Amatista. The Catholics have an ancient adobe chapel that gets a visit from a succession of random priests who conduct mass about every third Sunday. The other congregation is a group of nondenominational Protestants who meet in the back of Freddy Fernandez's barbershop. Freddy's barbershop sits right next to the Bird Cage Café, so it's certainly convenient. Freddy isn't really a pastor, but that's what Juanita calls him anyway.

"Pastor Freddy claims his son is practically a genius," Juanita told me. "Pastor says that's why Marco has trouble holding down a job. Not enough intellectual challenge. Freddy says Marco plans to make a fortune inventing his own cryptocurrency, as soon as he scrapes together enough real-world money to get started. I asked Marco about it when he first started working for me, and the boy tried to explain how cryptocurrency works, but it went straight over my head."

"I don't really understand how cryptocurrency works, either," I admitted.

"I think it's all a bunch of bosh," said Juanita. "As a favor to Freddy, I agreed to give Marco a chance, but he's the slowest, laziest dishwasher I've ever had. Still, he's lasted longer here than he usually does. I heard that Nancy Flynn's brother-in-law got him a job working on a concrete crew, and he lasted only three days before they fired him."

She broke off speaking when Chamomile came in from the dining room with a new batch of order slips.

"You have a key to your aunt's apartment?" Juanita asked. "It's a real mess, I'm afraid."

I held up the ring of keys that Mr. Wendell had handed off to me. Before her death, my aunt had helpfully labeled them. Unfortunately, about half of them were simply labeled "?"

I climbed the back stairs to my aunt's second-story apartment, Earp in tow. Halfway up the stairs, the pug overtook me. He was excited to be returning to his old environment. When I unlocked the door and switched on the light, he ran from room to room, searching for his former human companion. When he didn't find her, he returned to my side and howled until I found a bag of dog treats under the sink and gave him a whole handful. After that, he trotted over to his bed in the corner of the living room, made three rotations, and settled down to a light doze.

I wondered if Earp's search for Aunt Geraldine would be a regular returning-home routine for a while. Did dogs grieve? They must. I believed dogs felt something like love, so they must also feel the pain of separation. I decided to put off going back down to the rental car to retrieve my suitcases, for fear of waking up Earp. I'd get them later when I went back down to catch up with Juanita.

It was strange to be in Aunt Geraldine's house and know she was gone and never coming back. It was the little things that got to me: the half-finished Sudoku on the dining table, the slippers next to her bed, and the month-old TV guide sitting under the remote with Law and Order circled (notation: MUST WATCH!!!), and the Bachelor crossed out so vigorously that it was almost unreadable (notation: BRAIN ROT!!!).

I opened the refrigerator door and hastily closed it again. I made a mental note to buy gloves and a box of heavy-duty trash bags.

I kept an eye out the living room window on the parking spaces in front of the café, and by eight the cars had thinned out considerably. I snuck out, leaving Earp snoring in his bed. I hoped he wouldn't wake up, find that he was alone in the apartment, and start to howl again.

A gangly young man, about the same age as Chamomile, but not nearly so pretty nor industrious, was listlessly wiping down tables in the almost-empty dining room. He had to be Marco. I greeted him on my way to the kitchen, but he didn't bother to look up.

Juanita and Chamomile were alone in the kitchen, cleaning up the detritus of the dinner hour.

"How's Earp settling in?" Juanita asked.

"He looked all over the apartment for Aunt Geraldine. When he couldn't find her, he howled, but he's finally settled down. He went to sleep after I stuffed him full of dog treats."

"I'm sure he must miss her," said Juanita.

"I imagine he must."

"Otherwise, how are things going? This must all be a bit of a shock." Juanita made a sweeping gesture that seemed to take in all of Little Tombstone. I wasn't sure if she was referring to Little Tombstone's shocking state of disrepair or the fact that I now owned it all, down to every last loose shingle and bit of peeling paint.

Either way, the answer was still the same, so I said, "Yes, it is a bit of a shock."

"You plan to stay for a while?"

"I don't have any place else to go," I said. "It's a long story, and I don't have the strength to tell it right now, but Frank and I are getting a divorce."

"Oh, Emma."

"It's OK. It was my choice."

It had been my choice, but only after I'd found out what Frank and Shirley had been up to.

"I thought you had a good job in LA," Juanita said. "Your grandmother was very proud of your accomplishments. She was always saying, 'my granddaughter the screenwriter.'"

Nine years ago, I'd sold a script that had been turned into the sleeper hit of the year, and I'd been labeled the girl wonder of the screenwriting world, but since then, up until about six months ago, I hadn't sold anything else that had made it past the option stage.

I'd bring in a little from time to time from doing endless revisions on someone else's work. Butchering it, most of the time, if I'm going to be honest. Not that it was my fault that other people's nuanced and thoughtful stories ended up as unrecognizable bilge. I just did what I was told.

We'd lived off Frank's income, for the most part, a fact he was forever reminding me of. Then, when I'd finally sold my second screenplay, I'd foolishly handed the entire amount over to Frank to upgrade his office. I might as well have flushed that entire chunk of change right down the toilet.

"I'm in between jobs right now," I told Juanita. "That's what we like to say in LA when we're totally skint and have no idea where our next meal is coming from. It's less humiliating, somehow, than admitting you're trying to decide between a job cleaning bus station bathrooms or one that involves spending eight hours a day harassing people about the late payments on their leased furniture."

I'd been suddenly saved from a similar fate by the unfortunate demise of my Great Aunt Geraldine. With prudent management, it might not matter if I never worked again.

I suspected that Juanita had no idea that my Aunt Geraldine was a millionaire several times over. I couldn't fathom how my aunt had managed such a feat. I decided it might be best to downplay that aspect of my inheritance until I figured out where all the money had materialized from, and who else knew it existed.

"Is your situation really that bad?" Juanita asked.

"No, I exaggerate. Cleaning bus station toilets was never on the table. I'll be fine. Aunt Geraldine left enough to tide me over for a while," I said, "and to take care of some of the things around here that have gone to wrack and ruin. Plus, if my screenplay becomes another hit, I'll have back end coming to me."

"Back end?"

"They give you more if the movie turns a profit. It's a percentage."

"I'm relieved that Geraldine left you something to live on in the meantime," Juanita said. "I always got the impression that Geraldine was barely making ends meet."

My aunt was a crafty old biddy, letting her dearest friend believe she was on the brink of bankruptcy. Clearly, Juanita had no idea about my aunt's substantial stockpile.

"Make me a list of everything that needs fixing," I told Juanita, "and I'll get to them as soon as I can find a handyman type capable of taking on such a colossal task. I asked Hank for a list of repairs, but he seemed more concerned that I do something about the local influx of aliens."

"Ah, he told you about the aliens, did he?"

"Is he—?" I tried to think of a diplomatic way to ask if Hank had finally taken a plunge off the deep end. He'd been teetering on the tip of the diving board for years. "Hank's always been odd, but it used to just be conspiracy theories, strange inventions, and an unwavering confidence in the existence of chupacabras. Hank's not moved on to full-blown hallucinations, has he?"

"I don't think it's as bad as that," Juanita said. "Hank's not claiming to have actually seen aliens or been abducted by them or anything."

"Then why is he convinced that Little Tombstone's being overrun by extraterrestrials?"

"It's the lights. He's been seeing strange lights and attributing them to alien visitors," Juanita lowered her voice and dropped her gaze. "I'd think Hank imagined the lights, except that I've seen them too."

Chapter Five

"Lights?" I asked Juanita. "What kind of lights?"

"I've seen them three times, blindingly bright lights hovering over the ground. Sort of blueish." Chamomile had gone home, but Marco was still out in the dining room washing the tables at half speed, so Juanita kept her voice low. "Hank claims to see them practically every night, out in the field on the other side of the trailer court."

"There's nothing out there but sagebrush and cactus," I said.

I wasn't prepared to embrace Hank's assessment that Little Tombstone was experiencing an alien invasion; in fact, if Juanita hadn't been so quick to corroborate his story, I'd have dismissed his tale without a second thought.

"That's not all," said Juanita. "According to Hank, there are strange marks on the ground out where he thinks the lights are hovering."

"Are you and Hank the only ones who've seen the lights?" I asked.

"As far as I know, Hank and I are the only ones. Morticia, Ledbetter, and Chamomile all say they haven't noticed anything amiss. You couldn't see the lights from the trailer court itself, though, not unless you were outside peeking through a hole in the fence."

"When did you see these lights?"

"All three times I've seen them have been when I left the café late at night," Juanita told me. "I only noticed them because I'd parked over on the other side of the old motel to keep the spots out front freed up for customers."

"How late at night was it when you saw the lights?" I asked.

"Around 1:00 in the morning."

"Same as Hank?"

"Hank's seen lights even later. Two or even three AM."

"What about Katie?"

"Chamomile said she hadn't mentioned anything. Katie does leave for work very early. Five in the morning most mornings, but I guess by that time, the lights must be gone."

Later that night, as I lay in my Great Aunt Geraldine's bed, staring at the moonlit water stains on the ceiling where the roof had been leaking and listening to Earp snoring from his spot at my feet, I couldn't stop thinking about the strange lights and unexplained markings on the ground. I knew they couldn't possibly be the handiwork of aliens, but if little green men weren't visiting us from a galaxy far, far away, then who was?

The next morning I got up bright and early and had a hearty and nutritious breakfast consisting of stale All Bran washed down with a bottle of Ensure (vanilla), which were the only remotely edible things in the apartment unless I counted Earp's dog treats under the sink.

After I'd polished off a second bottle of Ensure (chocolate), and Earp had eaten an entire bowl of dog treats, I found a tablet of paper and a pencil and got to work organizing myself.

TO DO, I wrote in big, bold letters at the top of the blank page. I nibbled the tip of the eraser until I discovered that petrified rubber doesn't taste so good. Then I wrote:

#1: Buy Groceries. Dog food. Cleaning supplies.

Don't forget gloves. Ditto trash bags.

#2: Find Handyman.

#3: Go through Aunt Geraldine's things?

I got stuck on number three. I wasn't sure what to do with Aunt Geraldine's belongings. She might have left everything to me, but I couldn't help feeling that it wasn't quite right. Sure, Aunt Geraldine might have been angry at her daughter and granddaughters (although I'd never quite been clear on why they had such a rocky relationship), but, once her wrath had cooled, would she really have wanted them to have nothing besides a broken-down Oldsmobile, mismatched Tupperware, and a partial set of encyclopedias to remember her by?

I decided that I'd just throw out the obvious trash and box up anything that might have sentimental value. It wasn't like there weren't enough nooks and crannies around Little Tombstone to stash a few boxes of keepsakes.

I drove to the closest grocery store on the southern edge of Santa Fe. After I'd stocked up on food and cleaning supplies, I scavenged enough cardboard boxes to fill up the back of my rental car.

When I got back to Aunt Geraldine's, I added another item to the list.

#4: Buy car.

I'd inherited a running vehicle from Aunt Geraldine, but I was too scared to drive it. It was a 1957 Chevy pickup, and it had been all Aunt Geraldine had driven for as long as I could remember. Over the years, it had developed an increasingly long list of quirks. Even were I to succeed in getting it started, I was afraid of getting stranded along the side of the road without the intimate knowledge of its eccentricities necessary to get it running again.

After I'd cleaned out the refrigerator and filled it with groceries, I set to work on the rest of the house.

I was just removing about fifty years' worth of tax files—which I intended to examine later for insight into the source of Aunt Geraldine's wealth—from the filing cabinet in the back of the spare bedroom closet when there was a rattling at the door of the apartment. After whoever was out there didn't succeed in getting inside, they knocked vigorously, rattling the door against the deadbolt I'd engaged the night before.

There was no peephole in the door, so I demanded to know who it was before I opened it.

"It's Georgia! Open up!"

I opened the door and found my twin cousins, Freida and Georgia—second cousins, to be entirely accurate—standing impatiently on the landing outside.

Growing up, Georgia and Freida and I had spent a lot of time together at Little Tombstone, and since I'd been born just a month after the twins, we'd been expected to play nicely together—or else. I'd never been terribly fond of either of my cousins, but even when we were kids, Freida had been the twin to look out for.

Georgia would pick a fight with you if you so much as looked at her sideways, but she always fought fair. She never ambushed you from behind, and she never got anyone else to fight her battles for her.

Freida, on the other hand, was the type who'd skip the fight altogether and go straight to the higher-ups. I remember getting on Freida's bad side for some reason—I can't recall why—and she threw herself down in the dirt while she screamed like a banshee. When she was done messing up her pristine flowered dress, she'd even ripped the pocket off the skirt for dramatic effect. Then she'd run to my Grandma, sobbing her big blue eyes out and claiming that I'd knocked her down and torn her dress.

I'd gotten in terrible trouble for that, among innumerable other things that hadn't been my fault. The summer we'd all turned thirteen, though, Freida had done something I'd never been able to forgive her for.

My grandmother owned a spectacularly ugly vase that resembled a leering pufferfish with a hormone imbalance. It had once belonged to my great-great-grandmother, and despite its garishness, my grandmother loved the hideous thing.

One day, during one of my lengthy summer visits, I'd come into my grandmother's living room to find Freida holding the vase in her hands.

Freida had smiled sweetly at me, not breaking eye contact as she dropped the vase onto the floorboards. It had smashed to bits, of course, and as I stood there in horror, Freida had gone tiptoeing off, still smiling that sticky sweet smile of hers.

Freida must have alerted my grandmother to the broken vase, because a few minutes later, Grandma came in and found me stooped over the debris, trying to fit the poor pufferfish's smile back onto his bloated face.

I got the paddling of a lifetime. I tried to tell my grandmother that it wasn't me who'd broken the vase, but she didn't buy my story that Freida had done it on purpose, just to get me into trouble.

That was the thing about Freida: she'd do things so malicious that anyone who hadn't yet been the target of my cousin's wrath found it impossible to believe in her victims' protestations of innocence.

Freida invariably did her dark deeds with a saccharine smile on her face. I'd wondered more than once if my cousin Freida might not be seriously disturbed.

Freida, who waited impatiently outside the apartment door beside her sister Georgia, was smiling that saccharine smile now. I fought the impulse to slam the door in their faces. Freida was no less terrifying to me now than she'd been when we both were ten, although I was determined not to show it.

Georgia was scowling, but I wasn't scared of Georgia. Georgia had given up hitting people around the time we'd all become teenagers, although she had never shed her prickles and peevishness.

Besides, I couldn't blame Georgia for scowling. She'd always had a well-developed sense of justice and fair play, and I was acutely aware that my Great Aunt Geraldine's decision to leave me practically everything must have offended it. If I'd been in Georgia's place, I'd certainly have wanted to know why I'd been left nothing but a stack of antiquated encyclopedias.

The problem was, I was just as much in the dark as Georgia as to why Aunt Geraldine had decided to cut her daughter and granddaughters out of the will.

"You'd better come in," I said and stepped aside to let the twins into Aunt Geraldine's apartment.

Chapter Six

"You must be wondering why we're here," Freida began, still smiling that hideous fake smile of hers.

Actually, I wasn't wondering why. I was pretty sure my cousins were there because they'd recently found out they'd been cut out of Aunt Geraldine's will. What I wasn't sure of was what they intended to do about it.

My cousins, unlike Juanita, might be privy to just how much Aunt Geraldine had left me. Equally possible, since my aunt had omitted any mention of any of her considerable investments in the will, Georgia and Freida might have no idea that their grandmother had been loaded. I decided to keep quiet and let my cousins do the talking.

"We're contesting the will," Georgia said. "Someone was exerting undue influence over Grams when she had it rewritten."

"Who?" I asked. "Who was exerting undue influence?"

I was curious to know who this person was who might have talked my Great Aunt Geraldine into passing over her daughter and granddaughters and leaving everything to me. The only person I could think of who would even have that kind of clout with my aunt was Juanita, but I couldn't imagine her urging Aunt Geraldine to cut her offspring out of her will.

"It was you!" said Georgia, pointing an accusing finger at me.

"Me? I haven't seen Aunt Geraldine in person since my grandmother's funeral. I didn't even know she was sick. It was just as much of a shock to me as it was to you when I found out she'd left Little Tombstone to me."

They clearly didn't believe me. Georgia huffed through her nose like a bull pawing the ground in preparation for going after the matador. Freida stretched her smile a tiny bit wider— something I wouldn't have thought possible until she pulled it off.

My cousins didn't stay long after that. I offered to let them take a look through my great aunt's things and stake a claim to anything they wanted, but it appeared they were far more interested in getting their paws on the deed to Little Tombstone.

I was just suggesting that perhaps Freida might want to take away her grandmother's antique tea set when Earp emerged from the bedroom. He'd become a bit deaf, but I was still surprised that Georgia's pounding on the door earlier had not woken him up.

Now it appeared that he had spontaneously awakened from his midday doze. He stalked into the hallway and stood there, at a distance, bristling and snarling.

There were a great number of people who Earp disliked, but he usually limited his expressions of distaste to surly avoidance and the occasional disgruntled growl. I'd never seen him get so instantly worked up over a familiar person before. I went and grabbed him by the collar before he could do either of my cousins any actual damage.

"Hello, Earp," said Georgia, fearlessly approaching and giving the still-distraught Earp a perfunctory pat on the head. Earp ignored her and kept his eyes fixed on Freida.

Apparently, it wasn't both the twins that Earp wanted to tear to pieces. It was just Freida he heartily disliked.

Freida took Earp's aggression as their cue to leave.

"You'll be hearing from our lawyer," said Georgia.

I locked the door behind them, slid the deadbolt back into place, and tried to calm Earp down with a handful of dog treats, but he wasn't having it. For another ten minutes, he stood bristling, with his eyes glued to the door as if he expected Freida to come back through it at any second and visit unimaginable horrors upon us.

I dug through my handbag and found the card Mr. Wendell had given me the day before when he'd presented me with Aunt Geraldine's will.

I called the number, but it went to voicemail. Twenty minutes later, Mr. Wendell called me back.

"Your cousins have been by to see me," Mr. Wendell informed me before I'd even had a chance to explain why I was calling. "I informed them that it would be better for them to communicate with me via their legal representative, but my advice fell on deaf ears."

"I suppose they told you that they plan to contest the will."

"They did. I don't think you have anything to worry about. Your cousins appear completely unaware of the investment accounts your great aunt left you. However, they appear determined to contest the will and gain control of Little Tombstone. I can recommend a couple of competent probate lawyers—"

"Aren't you a competent probate lawyer?" I asked.

"I'm the executor. I also drafted the will at your aunt's request," said Mr. Wendell. "If your cousins contest the will on the basis of fraud or undue influence, it would be best for me to be seen as a disinterested outside party."

"Oh."

Mr. Wendell texted me the numbers of three probate lawyers in Santa Fe, but I lacked the determination to follow through on calling for an appointment. Nothing about the situation made sense to me, and I hoped time would illuminate the mystery of my great aunt's wealth and why she had left it all to me. Instead of calling a lawyer, I continued the long slog of clearing out Aunt Geraldine's overstuffed apartment.

Around eight, I realized I'd had nothing to eat since breakfast besides a jumbo bag of potato chips, so I went downstairs in hopes that there'd be a serving left from the supper special. I didn't want to trouble Juanita to cook me up something just as she was preparing to go home for the evening.

When I came into the kitchen, I observed Juanita and Chamomile huddled in whispered conference. I cleared my throat loudly, and Chamomile scuttled away.

"What was that about?" I couldn't resist asking.

"It's Marco," Juanita whispered, one eye on the door into the dish room. "Chamomile is convinced he's stealing money from the register."

"Why does she think that?"

"She saw him in the dish room, right after supper, counting out a wad of cash."

"Couldn't you compare the order slips with what's in the register?"

"That's what I intend to do," Juanita said grimly, "and if there's a discrepancy, I won't hesitate to fire him."

I sat in the empty dining room eating a plate of chicken enchiladas while Juanita sat at the cash register with the order slips from supper and an old-fashioned adding machine, calculating the day's earnings. Then she counted out what was in the register.

"It's all there according to the order slips, and it added up to about what I expected it to be," Juanita said in a low voice as she went past my table. "I don't know where he got the money."

"Do you suppose he's stealing Chamomile's tips?"

"Chamomile saw Marco with a thick stack of twenties. Nobody around here leaves twenties as tips."

After I'd polished off the enchiladas, I took my plate back to the dish room. Marco and Chamomile had both departed for the night, so I rinsed my plate and left it in the sink to be run through the sterilizer in the morning.

Juanita was putting on her jacket as I came back through the kitchen.

"I'm heading upstairs," I said. "Good night, sleep tight, don't let the bedbugs bite."

As it turned out, I was the one who almost got bitten, and by something considerably bigger than a bedbug.

Chapter Seven

As soon as I stepped into my aunt's apartment, I knew something was amiss. I hadn't left any windows open, yet I felt a cool breeze. I switched on the light and called out for Earp. I heard a dull thud as he jumped off the stepstool I'd left by the bed so he could coax his arthritic legs into making it up onto his favorite perch.

Earp was just emerging from the bedroom when something dark fluttered down from the light fixture which hung over the table in the kitchen dinette and headed for my face.

I screamed and waved my arms around. I hit something soft, and it fell to the floor.

The bat lay there, stunned for a few seconds. I didn't know what to do. Earp came over cautiously, barking anxiously at the creature that lay inert on the floor. I looked around for something to protect the bat from Earp and Earp from the bat. I found a plastic laundry basket on top of the washing machine, overturned it, and placed it over the bat like a cage.

The bat was safely contained, although I hadn't the slightest idea what I was going to do with it when it came to again. While waiting to see if the bat would revive, I went in search of how it had gotten into the apartment in the first place.

I did not have to look far. I was positive I'd closed all the windows when I went down to the café for supper, and they were all closed still. Technically. However, in the living room, which overlooked the street parking in front of the café, one window was missing most of the glass out of the bottom sash.

Before investigating further, I picked up the protesting Earp and carried him writhing and pawing to the bedroom and locked him in before he cut himself walking over shards of glass. Then I cautiously picked my way over to the window.

There was broken glass everywhere. In the middle of the rug was a large rock with a note securely knotted to it with a piece of neon green surveyor's string. I cut the string with a kitchen knife and carefully unfolded the note.

The note was handwritten in black permanent marker on a sheet torn from a yellow legal pad.

I read aloud to the empty room. "Get out of town before the flood comes." My voice was clear and steady, but my hands were shaking.

Meanwhile, Earp was throwing himself against the inside of the bedroom door and howling. I glanced over at the bat under the laundry basket and saw that it was stirring back to life.

I put down the note and went over to the bat under the basket. I stared at it for several minutes before I decided that this was all too much for me. I needed reinforcements.

I went out of the apartment, locking the door behind me, and crept downstairs. The lights were off on the ground floor, so I knew that Juanita had gone home.

It creeped me out to know that sometime while I'd been merrily chowing down on chicken enchiladas in the dining room, somebody had thrown a rock through my window, and no one had even noticed. I let myself out the back door, closing it soundlessly behind me. It was delusional to believe that if I were quiet enough, whoever was out there—if they still were—would not be able to see me, but I nevertheless kept as quiet as I could.

The lights in Morticia's Winnebago were off, and the little red Honda she drove was missing, so I decided she had gone off somewhere for the evening. It had never occurred to me to wonder about Morticia's private life, but now I was curious to know where she'd gone. Did she have friends in Amatista? A boyfriend, perhaps?

There was one light on in the trailer that Katie and Chamomile shared, but I figured it was only Chamomile who was still awake since Katie got up before the crack of dawn to go work at the post office. Chamomile did not seem like a good candidate to cope with bats.

There was a light on in Ledbetter's trailer. I decided he was my best bet. He was the biggest man I'd ever met in real life—and I mean muscular big, not like fat or anything—and he used to be in the marines, so I figured a little bitty bat trapped under a laundry basket wouldn't faze him, or at least he'd be too macho to admit it, if it did.

Ledbetter opened the door after the first knock and peered out into the darkness with his intense blue eyes.

"It's Emma," I said. "Geraldine's grandniece."

Ledbetter opened the door wider, and light streamed out the trailer door. I noticed that he'd grown a beard since I'd last seen him, and it only served to make him more intimidating, although, sadly, the effect of all that facial hair would likely be lost on the bat.

"Sorry to bother you," I said. "But there's a bat in Aunt Geraldine's apartment, and I'm afraid getting it out may be a two-person job."

"A bat?" Ledbetter echoed. "I hope you don't want me to kill it."

"No!" I said. "I don't want you to kill it. I just don't want it to be flying around the room and roosting on the chandelier."

"Oh." Ledbetter sounded relieved. "Sure, I can help you get it out of the apartment."

When we got upstairs to Aunt Geraldine's, I showed him the bat trapped under the laundry basket, but he seemed a lot more interested in the broken window.

"Someone threw a rock through it." I pointed to the rock still sitting on the living room rug. "It happened while I was downstairs eating supper at the Bird Cage."

Ledbetter picked his way through the broken glass and looked out the damaged window.

"They had to have been standing out in the middle of the street to throw it up here." He looked back at the rock. "Something that size," he continued, "would need a slingshot or a catapult unless the person who threw it was really jacked."

"Jacked?"

"You know—" Ledbetter flexed his biceps and veins stood out all over the place.

I stared up into his bright blue eyes. He didn't even blink.

"You didn't do it, did you?" I asked.

Ledbetter laughed. He never laughs. He stopped laughing when I handed him the note which had been tied around the rock.

"You should report this to the police," he said.

"What police? Does Amatista even have a police department?"

"Call the county sheriff's office in the morning," Ledbetter insisted. "Seriously, I mean it. Don't blow this off."

We got the bat out by sliding a flattened cardboard box underneath the laundry basket and carrying the whole thing, overturned basket and bat, gingerly down the stairs, and out the back door. After Ledbetter took the basket off, the bat fluttered away, hopefully to rejoin his bat family.

"Ledbetter," I said, as soon as the bat had disappeared into the darkness. "Is there something about Aunt Geraldine that nobody's telling me?"

Ledbetter and my aunt had been close in the years leading up to her death, although I'd never quite figured out why they'd hit it off. Maybe it was more a matter of proximity than anything. Neither of them ever seemed to leave Little Tombstone unless they absolutely had to.

Ledbetter nodded, then put his finger to his lips and said, "You'd better get something to cover up that window, or the bat will come back and bring fifteen of his closest friends with him.

"How about this?" I suggested, holding up the box we'd used to contain the bat in the laundry basket. "I know where Aunt Geraldine kept her duct tape."

Ledbetter followed me upstairs and taped the box to the window frame while I swept up the broken glass. Earp had settled down considerably, but he was still agitating to get out, so after I'd picked the last of the glass out of the carpet, I released him from detention in the bedroom.

He ran straight to Ledbetter and sniffed around his ankles before stalking over to his water dish and drinking noisily.

"Coffee?" I asked Ledbetter.

"Don't drink coffee. Makes me jittery."

"Tea?"

He shook his head.

"Water?"

Ledbetter accepted a glass of water and sat down at the dining table.

"I'll tell you everything I know about your Aunt Geraldine," he said. "I think you have a right to know."

I waited while he tossed back his water like it was a shot of whiskey.

"I suppose you must be wondering where your aunt got all that money."

I had been wondering that. I was also wondering how Ledbetter knew my aunt had made a killing, when even Juanita, who'd been my aunt's best friend for at least the last 40 years, seemed to be in the dark about Aunt Geraldine's wealth.

"I don't know where she got her original cash," Ledbetter continued. "She never told me, and I never asked, but about eight years ago, she came to me with $150,000."

"Came to you?"

"There's something you don't know about me, either. I'm not a struggling vet living off disability, although I can understand why people think so. Very few people know my real circumstances, and I'm happy to keep it that way."

I didn't know how to respond to that, so I didn't.

"I'm a stock trader," Ledbetter continued. "I make short term trades. I taught myself. I read a lot of books and did a lot of fake practice trades. I got good at it."

"How good?"

"I'm a multimillionaire."

I stared at him. He stared back, still not blinking. I wondered if the man slept with his eyes open.

"You're probably wondering why I still live in that old trailer?" Ledbetter asked.

I was wondering that.

"It's comfortable; nobody bothers me, and I can keep to myself," Ledbetter said. "It never was about the money, anyway. I just wanted to prove to myself that I could succeed at something."

"So you invested Aunt Geraldine's money for her?"

"Yes."

"There's something else I'm baffled about," I said. "Why did Aunt Geraldine leave everything to me?"

"She liked you," Ledbetter said.

"I know she liked me, but if that were the only reason, it would have made a lot more sense just to leave me a portion of her estate. My question is: why did she decide to leave my aunt and cousins nothing at all?"

"I might be able to shed some light on that," said Ledbetter. "I don't know if it was true or not, but your Aunt Geraldine believed that Abigail and her daughters were trying to get her declared incompetent and get power of attorney. Geraldine was convinced they suspected she was hiding money from them—which she was, of course—but I don't think they ever had a clue of how much. According to Geraldine, about the time she got sick, Abigail and the twins started getting the idea that Geraldine wasn't nearly as broke as she made herself out to be, and everything went downhill from there. They never did succeed in getting power of attorney, though."

"Was Aunt Geraldine showing any signs of dementia?" I asked. "Might she really not have understood what she was doing when she changed her will?"

"Absolutely not." Ledbetter shook his head so vigorously it diverted Earp's attention from the spot he'd been licking on the linoleum, and he trotted over and reared up with his paws on Ledbetter's massive calf. "Geraldine was sharp as a tack right up to the end," Ledbetter insisted.

"Then how were they proposing to get power of attorney?" I asked. "Doesn't a person need a doctor to sign off on that or something?"

"You do," said Ledbetter. "I suspect they'd found some unscrupulous physician who was willing to do it for a cut of the cash, but Geraldine went and foiled their plans by dying on them before they had a chance to carry out their scheme."

"No wonder Aunt Geraldine was so steamed," I said. "That explains a lot."

It explained a lot, but it didn't explain the rock through my window or where Aunt Geraldine had come up with the seed money to invest with Ledbetter. It certainly didn't explain those mysterious lights in the field behind the trailer court.

Ledbetter was standing up to leave. Earp whined and pawed at his shoes.

"One more thing," I said, "do you know anything about those lights that Hank keeps seeing? Do you think he's for real?"

"He may think he's for real," said Ledbetter. "I'm not saying Hank's hallucinating, but bear in mind that Hank Edwards also believes he has the finest collection of genuine stuffed chupacabras in the northern hemisphere."

I decided Ledbetter had a point. After he left, I double-locked the door and went to bed. I couldn't fall asleep. I kept imagining that whoever had thrown a rock through my window was standing down there on the street, watching my windows for signs of activity within.

After lying awake for over an hour, I remembered that my Aunt Geraldine had mentioned once that she occasionally slept with my late Uncle Ricky's antique pearl-handled revolver underneath her pillow.

"In case someone tries to rob me," she'd said, although at the time I couldn't imagine what Aunt Geraldine possessed that any self-respecting burglar would think worth carrying off. Even her TV predated the turn of the millennium. In hindsight, I wondered if Aunt Geraldine hadn't fallen into the habit of keeping large amounts of cash on the premises and lived in constant fear that someone would find out about it.

I rooted around in my aunt's nightstand and found the revolver hidden in the back of the bottom shelf.

I was afraid to touch the thing, so I removed it gently from the velvet-lined leather case and held it gingerly between my thumb and forefinger. I don't know how I managed to do it, but somehow my finger depressed the trigger. Fortunately, it wasn't loaded, but I was so shaken up by nearly shooting myself in the foot that I shoved the thing back in its case.

I told myself that whoever had thrown that rock through the window probably had no intention of inflicting bodily harm on me; they just wanted me out of Little Tombstone.

I carefully put the gun case back where I'd found it behind the stack of paperback thrillers in the bottom of the nightstand and finally fell into a fitful slumber.

Chapter Eight

The next morning, when I went down to the café and told Juanita and Chamomile what had happened, they both agreed with Ledbetter's advice that I should go to the police.

"With that broken-out window, I really do have to find a handyman," I said. "Do either of you know of anybody who might be interested?"

Juanita didn't, and neither did Chamomile. When I stuck my head into the dish room and asked Marco, he just moved his head a fraction of an inch to the left and then a fraction of an inch to the right, all the while deflecting my attempts to make eye contact. I took that as a "no."

I borrowed a black marker from underneath the register and went around to the recycling pile behind the motel for a piece of clean cardboard.

"Wanted," I wrote. "Man with carpentry, plumbing, and electrical experience." Then I wrote down my phone number. I stared at the sign for a minute, then put the letters HU in front of MAN, so it read "Wanted: Human." I wasn't very optimistic that I'd get any takers amongst the humans eating breakfast at the Bird Cage Café, but I was hopeful that maybe somebody would know somebody who knew an unemployed handyperson type.

As I was taping up my cardboard sign over the register, the door jingled, and a young man with wild curly red hair, a bushy red beard, and a large, threadbare backpack came into the café.

"You can seat yourself," I told him.

Chamomile was busy taking orders. The young man took off his backpack.

55

"Mind if I leave this here?" he asked me. I took the pack and put it behind the counter.

"You from Australia?" I asked. It was obvious from his accent, but I asked anyway.

"Yeah. I'm hitching cross-country. What's the chance I could work off my meal? You know, wash dishes or something?"

I looked him up and down. He was awfully skinny. I wondered how much of the time he spent walking along the side of the road waiting for some brave soul who hadn't watched too many movies about hitchhikers who turn out to be serial killers to pick him up. I decided to live dangerously and assume that this particular hitchhiker was not a serial killer. Or maybe it was the other way around, and it was drivers who picked up hitchhikers who turned out to be serial killers. For someone who worked in the movie industry, I was woefully ignorant of the hitchhiker/serial killer protocol.

"Do you happen to know anything about carpentry?" I asked the hitchhiker.

His name was Oliver, he told me. He was twenty-four. He had three brothers and one sister back home, all of whom worked for the family construction business. He'd be happy to do any little jobs we needed to have done in return for meals and a place to pitch his tent for a few nights.

"Perfect!" I told him. "I have a list, but first, you should get a good hot meal inside you."

As soon as I said it, I realized that it sounded just like something my grandmother would have said. Disconcerting, but compared to some of the other things my grandmother had said in her time, it could have been a lot worse.

After Oliver had gotten outside of a plate of Juanita's famous beef fajitas, I took him upstairs to look at my broken window.

"How did this happen?" Oliver asked.

"It's a long story," I said.

Actually, it was a short story, but I didn't want to tell it. My eyes involuntarily strayed toward the rock, sitting on top of the folded note next to the little ball of bright green surveyor's string on the coffee table.

"Did someone throw a rock through your window?"

I nodded. Oliver looked like he had lots more questions, but he didn't ask any of them. Instead, he inquired if I had a tape measure. I dug one out from the toolbox I'd discovered under the kitchen sink.

"You'll need to order a pane of glass, and I'll need some glazer's putty, but as soon as you have those things on hand, I can fix it easily," Oliver said as he handed me the measurements for the replacement pane.

"I can take you in to the Home Depot in Santa Fe this afternoon," I said. "And I'll look up glass places."

By the time we left for Santa Fe after lunch, Oliver had a lengthy list of materials to buy. I hoped he knew what he was doing, but I doubted he could make things worse even if it turned out he was bluffing about his carpentry skills.

I dropped Oliver off at Home Depot with his list and a wad of bills and loose change I'd scrounged from Aunt Geraldine's nightstand.

Oliver's backpack was still behind the counter at the Bird Cage Cafe, so I was pretty confident that I wouldn't come back and find out that he'd skipped on me.

While Oliver was shopping, I went to the Santa Fe County Sheriff's office and filed a report. The officer who filled out the paperwork for me said they'd try to send someone out in the next day or two "as staffing and time allowed," but I wasn't optimistic. There wouldn't be much to see when the officer got there, anyway.

When I returned, Oliver was waiting at the curb for me, a bulging bag in each hand and a couple of two-by-fours lying at his feet.

"Where are we going to put those?" I asked, pointing to the eight-foot lengths of lumber.

"We'll have to stick them out the window," he said.

I don't know how I managed to get out of Santa Fe without being pulled over for carrying an unsecured load, but, somehow, we made it back to Amatista without mishap. Oliver unloaded the car and immediately went to work repairing the broken-down step at the front of the café.

I went upstairs to let Earp out to do his business and almost tripped over my cousin Freida, who was sitting on the landing waiting for me.

"You changed the locks," she said.

I hadn't, but I figured that my Aunt Geraldine might have changed them during the whole power of attorney drama, so I didn't bother to dispute Freida's point.

"Why are you here?" I asked.

"I changed my mind."

"About what?"

"I want the tea set and a few other things."

I let Freida in and set to work wrapping up the tea set in newspaper while she went in search of a box of love letters my aunt and uncle had sent to each other during their courtship. It struck me as odd that Freida would want something so sentimental, but I'd offered for her to take anything of Aunt Geraldine's that she wanted, so I was in no position to question her choice.

Freida was in and out in half an hour. She went away with the tea set, the box of letters, and a cuckoo clock that my aunt had kept in the hall.

Before she went, she asked to see my Uncle Ricky's antique pearl-handled revolver.

"You're welcome to it," I told Freida, "You'll find it in the nightstand."

Freida retrieved the case from Aunt Geraldine's bedroom. She unfurled a paper towel and gingerly removed the gun from its case.

"This thing is filthy," Freida said, wrinkling her nose like a fastidious five-year-old smelling a run-over skunk through the open window of a car.

It didn't look any filthier than anything else in the apartment, which, admittedly, did seem to be coated with a layer of dust and grime. Perhaps, Great Aunt Geraldine's eyesight had deteriorated considerably during her last years, or perhaps, she'd simply stopped caring about trivial tasks like dusting.

"Oh, I don't know," I protested, "it's not that bad."

"No, seriously, take a closer look," Freida said, suddenly chummy.

She thrust the gun toward me, and I had no choice but to take it.

I pretended to look at it and handed it back to Freida, but instead of taking it out of my hand, she held out the case.

I placed the revolver inside the antique velvet-lined case, and Freida snapped it shut.

"I've changed my mind," she said. "After seeing it, I don't think I really want it after all."

When Freida left, I let Earp out of the bathroom where I'd barricaded him. He'd made a terrible ruckus the whole time my cousin had been there, which had hampered conversation, not that I cared to chat with Freida anyway. Earp popped out of the bathroom door like the cork out of a champagne bottle and ran around the apartment, sniffing everywhere Freida had been until he'd reassured himself that she was really gone.

Downstairs, I could hear hammering. My Australian hitchhiker was certainly earning his keep. I decided to go next door and see if there were any urgently needed repairs at the Curio Shop or the Museum of the Unexplained before my itinerant handyman moved on.

It had been years since I'd been inside the Museum of the Unexplained, but the only thing that appeared to have changed was that everything was coated in a slightly thicker layer of dust.

The featured display in the jumbled gallery was a family of chupacabras under glass. Both my grandmother and Aunt Geraldine had been adamant that the chupacabras were hoaxes, the work of a talented and highly creative taxidermist. Hank, on the other hand, was completely convicted of their authenticity.

"Hank?" I called out.

I wondered how often Hank had visitors to the Museum of the Unexplained. It was a good thing—at least for Hank—that his rent was purely symbolic. When I caught Hank in a good mood, I intended to try and pry out of him how he'd come to such a generous arrangement with my aunt.

I'd momentarily toyed with the possibility that Hank and my Great Aunt Geraldine had been carrying on an affair behind everyone's back, but then I'd gotten a close-up view of Hank and eliminated that as a possibility. There was no way that Hank Edwards was sufficiently hot stuff to inspire his landlady to give him—for all practical purposes—free rent for life. My Great Aunt Geraldine might have been an eccentric, but she'd not been blind, deaf, and deprived of her sense of smell.

Hank shuffled out from his living quarters in the back of the Curio Shop. The Curio Shop was connected to the Museum of the Unexplained by a large arched opening. Hank held onto the archway to steady himself.

"What do you want?" Hank asked. His clothing was rumpled, and his long unwashed gray hair was matted down on one side like he'd been asleep for the last nine hours. He smelled of whiskey, stale cigar smoke, and bacon grease.

I suspected that Hank was just getting out of bed. Maybe that was why Hank kept seeing unexplained lights. He was staying up all night, drinking hard liquor, and working himself into a paranoid frenzy.

Our alien invasion might be easily eradicated by the administration of a good sleeping pill, not that Hank was likely to visit a sleep clinic. Hank was deeply suspicious of the "Medical Industrial Complex" and "Big Pharma." According to him, everyone in the medical professions was conspiring to perniciously poison the entire US population for profit.

"I have someone here doing some repairs," I told Hank. "I was just checking to see if there was anything you were desperate to have fixed right away."

Hank stared around the museum. I was guessing there were dozens of things that needed repairing, but it was nearly impossible to tell because of the collection of valuable and not-so-valuable artifacts that covered every surface.

"You done anything about them aliens yet?" Hank demanded.

"I'm looking into it," I told him.

"No, you're not."

"I am. I really am," I insisted. "I've been asking around."

"Asking who?"

"People who live around here."

"They're lying," Hank said. "They're all lying. They call me crazy, but they're the ones who—"

"Juanita told me she's seen the lights. Do you think she's lying?"

"Juanita said that?" Hank looked genuinely shocked.

"She says she's seen strange lights on three separate occasions," I told Hank. "I really am serious about getting to the bottom of this. Did you see the lights again last night?"

"I was out last night."

"Out?"

Hank remained silent. He obviously didn't want to tell me where he'd been. I decided not to press the point.

"Something interesting happened yesterday evening," I said, watching his expression closely. "Someone threw a rock through my window with a threatening note attached."

"I knew that already," he said, his expression betraying nothing.

"How?"

"Katie told me when she came by with my mail."

"Oh," I said.

I wondered how Hank had talked Katie into personally delivering his mail when everyone else had to go down to the post office to pick up theirs. After that, I moved on to wondering how Katie knew about that rock through my window.

I decided that Chamomile must have told her. Probably everyone in Amatista knew by now. I let the subject drop. "So, you don't want me to send the repair guy over here?" I asked Hank.

He grunted, which I took to be a "yes." I started to leave, but halfway out the door, I turned back.

"Do you think the lights will appear tonight?" I asked.

"Maybe. Maybe not."

"Do you have a pen and paper?"

After I'd written down my number, I thrust it into Hank's hand. "The next time you see those lights, I want you to call me. It doesn't matter what time it is."

After I was done talking to Hank, I went and knocked on the door of Ledbetter's trailer. Nobody answered. Morticia's car was gone again, or maybe she'd never returned. I knew that Chamomile was inside the café, and Katie was still on her mail route. The place was deserted.

I was suddenly unbearably tired. What little sleep I'd gotten the night before had been fitful. I decided to go upstairs for a nap. I drifted off to sleep on the couch, Earp snuggled up next to me.

Both Earp and I were jolted awake by a relentless banging on the door.

Chapter Nine

The banging continued. Earp bolted off the couch, raced to the door, and hurled himself at it, barking frantically until I sat up, momentarily confused about where I was.

"Coming," I shouted in the direction of the banging.

Oliver stood outside the door, completely drenched in muddy water. Juanita stood beside him, also covered in mud, but only from the knees down.

"What happened?" I asked.

"You'd better come and have a look," Juanita said.

I followed Oliver and Juanita down the stairs and out the back door to the trailer court. There was a geyser erupting out of the ground next to Ledbetter's trailer.

"Any idea where the main shutoff is?" I asked Juanita.

"We've been there already. Somebody hacked the handle off, so it can't be turned."

"Surely, with a wrench—" I suggested.

"Tried that," said Oliver. "Someone sawed the handle off and then took a blow torch to it so that the valve is now frozen in the open position."

"Why would—" I was about to say, "why would anyone do that?" when I remembered the note which had been hurled through my window the day before.

"This must be the promised flood," I said.

"What promised flood?" Juanita raised her eyebrows.

"I showed you the note," I said to Juanita.

Oliver looked confused, but he quickly refocused on the crisis at hand.

"There's nothing more I can do," Oliver said. "You'd better call someone."

"Who do I call?" I looked over helplessly at Juanita, but she already had her phone to her ear.

Five minutes later, the mayor of Amatista showed up to assess the situation.

Nancy Flynn had been the mayor of Amatista for the last decade at least, mostly because nobody else wanted the job. Nancy was mid-sixties, thin as a rake and tough as nails. She owned the ranch that backed up to the vacant land attached to Little Tombstone. In other words, she was now my closest neighbor.

Nancy tore up in her enormous extended cab Chevy pickup and skidded to a stop right in the roadway. She jumped out and came running over.

Nancy didn't greet us, or offer advice, she just took over. She got on the phone with Tim, whoever Tim was, and told him to go to the pump house at the well and shut off the water system for the whole village.

"Do you know a good excavator?" she asked, focusing on none of us in particular. I wondered if she'd not yet heard the news that I was the new proprietress of Little Tombstone.

I waited for Juanita to answer, but when she didn't, I said, "No."

"My brother-in-law has a backhoe," Nancy said. "As soon as the system drains, you'll need to dig down to the pipe and fix the leak."

That seemed like stating the obvious, but I wasn't about to turn down the offer of a man with a backhoe, so I just said that sounded good to me.

"How did this happen?" Nancy asked, a deep furrow forming on her weather-beaten forehead.

"I don't know," I said, "but I have reason to believe someone did it on purpose."

"Why would anyone do a fool thing like that?"

"I don't have any idea who it was or what they were trying to accomplish," I told her.

That was pretty much a lie. I did know what they were trying to accomplish. The note thrown through my window had made the wishes of whoever had threatened the flood abundantly clear. Someone wanted me gone from Little Tombstone.

Nancy didn't let the subject go until she'd gotten the complete story of my inheriting Little Tombstone—which she appeared to know already—and the threatening note tied to the rock thrown through my window—which she appeared to be hearing about for the first time.

She listened to my story, but she didn't offer up any theories about who might do such a thing, she just told us to go inside and fill containers with water before the system drained and then hurried off to go door-to-door in the village telling everyone else to do the same. The entire village of Amatista—at least those without their own private wells—were going to be out of water until we got our problem fixed.

After I'd filled every container I could find, I went out back to see how the gusher on the trailer court was doing. There was still water coming out, but it had stopped erupting like Old Faithful.

While I was standing there, helplessly staring at the muddy mess, Ledbetter, wearing head-to-toe black leather, pulled up on his motorcycle. The bad-boy effect was somewhat diluted by the kale, leeks, and a new toilet bowl brush peeking out of the grocery sack tucked into his saddlebag.

"What happened?" Ledbetter asked.

"I'm not sure, but it looks like whoever wrote that menacing note made good on their threat. I'm sorry, but I think we're going to have to have your trailer moved to a different spot while they replace the section of damaged pipe."

"How did someone manage to break a buried pipe without anyone noticing?" Ledbetter wondered aloud.

I shook my head. I didn't know, but I suspected that once the damaged section was dug up, it might become more apparent how the culprit had managed to create such a mess.

"You didn't notice anything earlier, did you?" I asked Ledbetter. "Have you been gone all day?"

"I left around ten. Morticia's been gone since Thursday. She went to Phoenix to see her sister."

"And Katie left for work early this morning?"

"I assume so. She leaves around five AM every day but Sunday and Monday."

"Chamomile might have seen something," I pointed out hopefully. "She must take an extended break between lunch and supper, and she might have gone back to her trailer."

I went inside the Bird Cage Café, but even though it was time for supper, the place was deserted. I found Juanita out front, fashioning a large CLOSED sign from a couple of fruit boxes and a pair of old sawhorses.

"Where's Chamomile?" I asked Juanita.

"I let her leave since supper isn't going to happen. She said she was running up to Santa Fe to do a little shopping."

"And Marco?"

"He called in sick today, or rather Pastor Freddy called in for him. I was irritated, but I guess it doesn't matter now."

Our conversation was interrupted by the arrival of Nancy's brother-in-law with his backhoe. He pulled his truck around the side of the café and got out to survey the situation.

"What do you think?" I asked as I came up behind him. He was standing next to Ledbetter, who'd been joined by Oliver. They stood staring at the muddy pond which surrounded Ledbetter's trailer.

"Name's Jimmy," Nancy's brother-in-law said, extending his hand to me. "You must be Emma."

I said I was indeed Emma and asked him if he thought Ledbetter's trailer ought to be moved.

"There's a couple of empty slots down at the end," I pointed out.

Jimmy offloaded his backhoe and then set to work unhooking his utility trailer so that he could attach his truck to Ledbetter's ancient Airstream.

While Jimmy was moving Ledbetter's trailer, Nancy came back and waved Jimmy over to her pickup. Jimmy got into the passenger seat, and they sat inside for a while. It looked like they were arguing about something. At last, Jimmy opened the passenger side door of Nancy's pickup.

"I don't know why you're asking me to do this," I heard him say as he climbed down. "It makes no sense to wait. We need to get the water back on as soon as possible. I'll start working now, and I won't quit until I'm too tired to go on."

I couldn't hear what Nancy said back. After that, Nancy drove off, and Jimmy went back to work.

As I stood watching Jimmy attempt to maneuver his pickup truck through the mud without getting stuck, I remembered that Earp hadn't had his supper, so I went back inside.

I stayed out of Jimmy's way after that, although I'd peek out of a window overlooking the trailer court from time to time to assess his progress. He worked well into the night. By the time Ledbetter's trailer was successfully transferred to an empty slot at the other end of the trailer court, it had been dark for a while. Another pickup arrived with a friend of Jimmy's—I assumed—who brought a pair of bright utility lights like those used by road construction crews. Jimmy set these up to shine on the area he was digging and set to work unearthing the damaged section of pipe.

When I woke up in the morning, there was a large muddy hole where the pond had been. The backhoe was sitting idle and not a soul to be seen. I gave Earp his breakfast and made myself a cup of coffee using water from an old milk jug I'd filled the afternoon before.

I put a leash on Earp—which he vigorously objected to, but I did not relent—I didn't want him falling into the hole. I held Earp's leash in one hand and my coffee in the other and went downstairs to look at the hole in the ground while Earp answered the call of nature.

After watering an errant tumbleweed, Earp strained at the leash and was so difficult to control that I almost spilled my coffee. I went as close to the hole as I dared without giving Earp an opportunity to dash into it. A length of pipe about six feet long lay on the ground beside the hole. I set my coffee down on an overturned bucket and picked up the piece of pipe, further exciting Earp. He seemed to think it was all some kind of delightful game of tug-of-war.

The piece I held in my hands was obviously the damaged section cut from the pipe removed from the ground, and it didn't take long to discover the source of the leak. Several round holes about an inch in diameter were punched in the pipe at random. Toward the middle of the damaged section, multiple holes had been punched so close together that the pipe was nearly severed.

Earp took advantage of my preoccupation to jerk sharply on his leash and slip from my grasp. Two seconds later he was sliding down the sloped sides of the hole. He reached the bottom and sniffed around, barking excitedly. Then Earp began to dig at the edge of a muddy puddle with such singleness of purpose it would have put a reporter investigating a shady congressional candidate to shame.

I didn't bother with trying to pull Earp out. He hadn't injured himself during his descent into the hole, and it wasn't likely to cave in on him, so I decided to let him have his fun. I retrieved my coffee and sat down on the edge of the hole to watch.

"What's he digging for?" a voice said behind me.

I turned my head. It was Oliver. He'd spent the night on the floor in the dining room of the Bird Cage. The trailer court, which would normally have been a perfectly adequate place to pitch a tent, was now a mudflat.

"I haven't the slightest idea," I said.

Oliver sat down beside me, and we both silently watched Earp until he managed to unearth his treasure.

"I hope that's not what I think it is," said Oliver, as Earp finally managed to pull the object he'd been trying to extricate from the earth free.

Earp stood protectively over his precious find.

The pug had just dug up a human skull.

Chapter Ten

I stared at the skull. Oliver stared at the skull. Then we turned and stared at each other. Oliver got up and climbed into the hole with a shovel that had been left leaning against the backhoe. Earp stayed beside the skull, standing guard. I hoped he wouldn't decide to start using the skull as a chew toy.

I slid down into the hole after Oliver and took the shovel. I gingerly poked around the area where Earp had unearthed the skull. I'd been working at carefully removing the mud around what looked suspiciously like it might turn out to be a rib cage when the arrival of Jimmy halted my progress.

"What is that?" he said, pointing at the skull. He couldn't get close enough to it to get a better look because Earp inserted himself between the skull and Jimmy and growled.

"It's a skull," I said. "And it looks very much like the body that went with it is still down here."

"You'd better stop digging," said Jimmy. "If there really is a body down there, we'd better alert the authorities."

That seemed like sensible advice, so I took it. The dispatcher at the Santa Fe County Sheriff's Office promised that someone would call me right back. Within fifteen minutes, I was on the phone with the Sheriff himself, who informed me that he'd come out personally.

By lunchtime, the trailer court was cordoned off with yellow crime-scene tape and swarming with people.

I expected Nancy Flynn to show up in her capacity as mayor, but she didn't. I had Juanita try calling her, but it went to voicemail.

Before the police arrived, Jimmy had done a rush job of getting a new section of pipe put in, so Amatista had water again, although the pipe was still exposed, and the hole in the middle of the trailer court was bigger than ever.

By the time evening came, the digging had stopped. Two almost-complete skeletons lay on a big blue tarp behind Morticia's motor home.

"There seem to be a few pieces missing," Officer Reyes, the man in charge, told me.

"I might be able to help you with that," I said. "It seems our dog here has been digging up bones from time to time. We all thought he was getting them from the cemetery up on the hill, but maybe that's not it at all."

I went in search of the banana box of miscellaneous bones. I located it in room two of the motel just as Morticia had informed me I would.

"How old do you think these skeletons are?" I asked Officer Reyes after I'd presented him with the box of bleached extras.

"I have no idea, other than it has to have been at least a few years for there to be nothing left but bones."

"Will there be an investigation?" I asked.

"I'm sure there will be," he said. "Although it may turn out that it's just a very old gravesite that whoever built this place was unaware of." He lowered his voice. "I'd suggest you quiz all the old-timers around here and see what you can find out for yourself. Given how long these bodies have probably been in the ground, I doubt an investigation into their identities is going to be a priority."

The authorities took away all the bones. They even took away the banana box. Somebody took down the yellow tape. Jimmy filled in the hole, loaded up his backhoe, and left.

Ledbetter's trailer stayed in the slot where it had been moved to give the fill dirt in the hole a chance to settle.

That evening after the supper rush was over, Juanita, Chamomile, Oliver, and I stood in the kitchen of the Bird Cage Café and tried to make sense of it all.

"It's almost as if someone wanted those graves to be discovered," Juanita said.

I was doubtful.

True, the timing of the tampering with the water system was suspect, but how would whoever wanted me out of Little Tombstone know there were bodies buried underneath the trailer court unless that person had been involved in putting them there? And if they did know there were bodies, how would their discovery serve to drive me out?

"Who's lived the longest in Amatista?" I asked Juanita.

"My mother," Juanita said. "She was here from 1960 until just a few years ago when she went into the nursing home. Hank came in the late 60s, so he's been here a while, too."

"What about Ledbetter and Morticia?" I asked.

"I think Ledbetter's been here for eight years, and Morticia came the year after Ledbetter."

I decided that I'd leave looking into Ledbetter and Morticia until later.

Juanita's mother, Florenza Hernandez, was in a memory care center in Santa Fe. Grandma Flo's mind wasn't what it used to be. It wasn't that she'd lost her memory completely, according to Juanita, it was just that her attachment to reality came and went at regular intervals.

I'd go and visit Grandma Flo the next chance I got, I decided, but first, I'd have a nice long chat with Hank.

It was late. I was tired. I wasn't up to a nice long chat with Hank without a good night's sleep, so I decided to leave interrogating Hank about the possibility of sinister goings-on in Little Tombstone's past until tomorrow.

Hank had other ideas.

Chapter Eleven

Shortly after one in the morning, I was jolted awake by the ringing of my phone. My first thought was that whoever had sabotaged the water system was calling to issue another ultimatum, but it was just Hank.

"I seen 'em!" he said.

"The lights?"

I switched on the lamp and sat on the edge of the bed, rubbing my eyes. Earp grumbled in his sleep. All I wanted to do was switch the light back off and pull the covers over my eyes, but instead, I pulled on my aunt's woolly bathrobe over my flannel pajamas and put on my sturdiest shoes.

Then I crept down the stairs to the café dining room. I stood there with the light off and tried to decide whether or not to wake up Oliver.

"Emma?" I heard Oliver say from the darkness.

"Yeah," I said. I was trying to decide how to break it to my Australian hitchhiker that I wanted him to accompany me on a nocturnal hunt for alien life without sounding completely deranged when Oliver switched on the light.

I stared at him. I couldn't stop. He'd shaved off his beard and cut his hair. He looked like a different person.

"Emma?" he said.

I tried to think of something intelligent to say. All I could think of was that he was much better looking under all that facial hair than I'd imagined.

"Emma?" he said again.

"Has Hank happened to mention that he believes we are experiencing an alien invasion?" I said.

"Hank?"

"From the Curio Shop."

"Old man who smokes the cigars and is perpetually blotto? Looks like a mad scientist?"

"He's the one. Has he talked to you about aliens?

"No. We did have one conversation while I was trying to get his kitchen faucet to stop leaking, but that was about whether NASA is in league with the Illuminati. Hank thinks so. I don't."

"Well, Hank is firmly convinced we've got extraterrestrial visitors. He just called me insisting that there are strange lights in the field behind the trailer court, and he wants me to have a look."

"I'll come with you," Oliver said without being asked. "I'll get my torch."

We went out the back door as soundlessly as we could. There was a full moon overhead. Oliver left his flashlight off. We walked out to the road that bordered Little Tombstone and led up to Nancy Flynn's ranch and the Amatista cemetery.

We'd only walked down the road a few yards when we came to a point where the back fence of the trailer court was no longer blocking our view.

There really were lights. Hank was not hallucinating.

Just as Hank had described them, they were bright and blueish, in four sets of three, spaced unevenly and appearing to be suspended above the ground.

Oliver and I stood still, looking at the lights.

"I guess Hank isn't crazy," I whispered.

"Oh, Hank's completely crackers," said Oliver, "but it seems he's not hallucinating."

"What do you think?" I said. "I want to get closer."

The lights were at least three football-field lengths away.

"I don't believe in aliens," Oliver said.

"Me neither," I answered, although, if I'm going to be honest, I'd never come closer to believing in alien life forms than I did at that moment.

"If they aren't aliens, then they must be human," Oliver said, "and people would be expecting other people to approach from the road. How about we take the long way around?"

The land behind the trailer court was littered with boulders, sagebrush, cactus, and tumbleweeds. It wasn't nearly as flat as it looked in the daylight. We proceeded in silence for a while, periodically stumbling down into dips and going behind large boulders that obscured our view of the lights. I thought I made out movement on the ground as if there were people or animals under the lights, but it was still too far away to be sure. Occasionally, the wind would carry faint noises from the direction of the lights. As we got closer, I heard voices shouting indistinctly to one another, and at least one engine running, although it seemed to be turned off from time to time.

"I think they're digging with a backhoe or something," I told Oliver.

He didn't offer a dissenting opinion, but that may just have been because he was too busy trying to avoid running into any prickly pear. We'd shrunk the distance between us and the lights in half when we came to a small arroyo. Oliver slid down first, but I hesitated on the edge.

"I can't see where I'm going to land," I hissed down to him. "Turn on your flashlight."

"They might see the light," Oliver hissed back. "Just come down where I did, and you won't hit anything."

He was wrong.

Chapter Twelve

Oliver insisted that if I followed his path, I would come safely to rest at the bottom of the small arroyo that stood between us and the mysterious lights.

I had a little battle with myself and then launched myself down the slope. I'd started my slide in the same spot as Oliver, but I must have veered a little to the right because I came to rest against a barrel cactus.

I screamed bloody murder. I don't know what it feels like to be murdered, but at that moment, I felt like I was being stabbed to death with a thousand tiny knives.

I screamed some more, and Oliver turned on the flashlight.

"It's bad," he said as he illuminated my lower legs. I looked down. At least two dozen barrel cactus spines were sticking out of my knees and on either side of my lower legs. The right leg was worse than the left, which only had a couple of spines lodged in it.

"Do you think you can walk?" Oliver asked me.

I took a couple of cringing steps.

"I think if I can get out of this arroyo, I can make it back to Little Tombstone."

"I think you need to go to the emergency room."

"For cactus spines?"

Oliver didn't bother arguing with me. He went ahead of me up the sloping dirt wall of the arroyo and pretty much pulled me up after him. Before we started the long, painful slog through the sagebrush, I looked back in the direction of the lights.

"The lights are gone," I said. "Do you think whoever it was got scared off when I screamed?"

"You scared off anything with ears in a 30K radius with all that screaming," Oliver said.

It took us forever to make it back to Little Tombstone, and when we got there, I didn't attempt to climb the stairs. I dropped onto the floor right there in the dining room and sent Oliver in search of the first aid kit Juanita kept in the kitchen.

He came back with the kit and found a pair of tweezers. I took them out of his hand and set to work, trying to get the cactus spines out. Tears were streaming down my cheeks, but I kept going until I'd removed all of the spines except for two that had broken off.

"You're tough," Oliver said.

"Am I?" I didn't feel very tough. "I'll go to the walk-in clinic in Santa Fe tomorrow and have them dig these last two out of my leg. It's hopeless trying to get them out with these tweezers."

"Want me to drive you?"

"I'd really appreciate that, and after that, maybe we can go out and look at the spot where we saw the lights."

I didn't sleep much that night. Somehow, with a lot of help from Oliver, I managed to make it up the stairs to bed. Earp barely acknowledged my arrival home, and Oliver's presence didn't even seem to register.

I took some aspirin in hopes of cutting the pain, but it wasn't enough. Finally, after lying there for an hour, I got up and went into the bathroom. When I looked at myself in the mirror, I was startled to see multiple scratches on my cheeks. I looked like I'd tangled with a bobcat. After staring in horrified fascination at my war wounds in the mirror, I hobbled to the kitchen and made myself a cup of tea.

Earlier, I'd found a box of old scrapbooks and photo albums in the back of one of the closets, but I hadn't had time to look at any of them. I couldn't sleep anyway, so now seemed an ideal time to go through them.

I started with a small notebook off the top of the stack. It didn't prove very interesting, just the record from some yard sale back in June of 1992. A bunch of items were listed: Cuckoo clock –20, Antique sewing machine –50, copper boiler –36. Many items were identified simply by initials with numbers after them. This went on for pages.

I moved on to a scrapbook. It was full of newspaper clippings. They'd been added over a long period of time, perhaps a span of a decade or so from the mid-1980s to the mid-1990s, and the only unifying theme seemed to be local history.

There was one article about the derelict amethyst mine, which closed in the 1960s and which was responsible for the town of Amatista's name. There was another about Amatista being home to New Mexico's first lady physician in the 1880s (apparently, the lady doctor wore a gent's suit so convincingly that the local populace had only discovered they'd not been treated by a man after she herself fell deathly ill). Towards the back of the scrapbook was a series of articles about a stagecoach robbery.

According to the articles, back in 1910, a stagecoach carrying mail to Santa Fe had been robbed by two outlaws who murdered the stagecoach driver and made off, not with the mail, but with a consignment of gold coins the stagecoach had been transporting. The outlaws had been caught within days, not far from the village of Amatista, but before they were captured, they'd succeeded in stashing the gold somewhere. One of the robbers had died in prison, and the other had been eighty and in poor health by the time he'd been released. Whether the surviving outlaw had succeeded in eventually retrieving his ill-gotten gains was uncertain.

According to one article, it had been a major local hobby for a while to go out with a metal detector and a shovel and try to find that fortune in old gold coins. There was even an article featuring a picture of my Great Uncle Ricky wandering around in the sagebrush with his metal detector in front of him. The headline read, "Local Man Looks for Treasure."

Tucked into the page containing that clipping was a crude map.

The map consisted of several sheets of graph paper taped together with yellowed and brittle tape. I gingerly unfolded the papers and tried to make sense of the diagram. The buildings of Little Tombstone, the road to Nancy Flynn's ranch, and the cemetery were all labeled. Even the arroyo I'd fallen into earlier in the night was shown by a pair of faded squiggly parallel lines.

A number of the squares on the graph paper map had been colored in, some in red and some in yellow. Clusters of colored-in squares were labeled with what I took to be a date. In the middle of one of the clusters of yellow squares was a messy star drawn in black ink and the numbers 1/23/92, which I took to mean January 23, 1992.

I stared down at the messy map on the table. I looked again at the article showing my late Uncle Ricky and his metal detector. I was convinced that I was looking at my Uncle Ricky's treasure map, but what did the star mean? Did it mean that he'd found what he was looking for? Had my Uncle Ricky really found a fortune in gold?

I'd been seven in 1992. I tried to remember if my Uncle Ricky had still been alive when I was seven. I didn't think so.

I didn't waste time trying to sift through Aunt Geraldine's things for some record of his death. Instead, I fired up my laptop and searched for Uncle Ricky's date of death. It took me about ten minutes and several false leads to find it, but when I succeeded, I was in for a bit of a shock. Richard Norton Montgomery, born November 13, 1928, died July 7, 1991.

If that star meant someone really had found that stash of stolen gold, it hadn't been my Uncle Ricky, and if it hadn't been my Uncle Ricky than it must have been my Aunt Geraldine. It was finally clear to me how she had managed to amass a fortune and keep it hidden from everyone.

More than likely, she'd even hidden it from the taxman.

Chapter Thirteen

The next morning, I had a terrible time getting out of bed. Everywhere I'd been skewered with a cactus spine was red and swollen. The locations of the two spines that remained in my leg throbbed with pain. Earp was agitating to go out, so I dragged myself downstairs and let Earp outside to do his business in his usual spot by the dumpster out back of the café.

I'm generally the responsible sort who would never think of leaving poop unscooped, but that morning it was beyond my capabilities. I lured Earp back to me with a dog treat and went inside in search of Oliver.

Before I found Oliver, Juanita found me.

"What in the world happened to you?" Juanita said, horrified.

I hadn't looked in the mirror yet that morning, but, based on what I'd looked like the night before, I wasn't surprised that Juanita was shocked.

"I may have tangled with a barrel cactus in the wee hours of the morning. Is Oliver around?"

"What were you doing anywhere a barrel cactus could get at you in the wee hours of the morning?" Juanita demanded.

"Hank saw lights again," I told her.

"And you went chasing off after them on your own?"

"I wasn't on my own. Oliver went with me."

This did not seem to reassure Juanita in the least. "About Oliver—" she said, but she broke off when the front door jingled, and the man in question walked into the dining room.

"You ready to go to the clinic?" he asked me.

Earp, who had been sniffing around under the tables in hopes of finding something edible, left off his search for abandoned morsels and came over to Oliver and leaned against his leg until Oliver bent down and scratched him behind the ears.

"You mind taking Earp upstairs?" I asked Oliver. "I don't think I have the strength. His food is under the kitchen sink, and my purse is on the dining table. If you don't mind, I'd also like to have the jacket that's hanging on the hook by the front door."

I didn't remember until it was too late that I'd left the graph paper map I'd discovered the night before laying spread out on the table next to my purse.

It was a very quiet, awkward drive to the clinic. I kept glancing over at Oliver, sitting at the wheel of my rental car, and thinking how green his eyes were and how perfect his nose was. After that, I alternated between watching the play of the tendons in his forearms as he turned the steering wheel and wondering if he'd taken a close look at the map I'd left sitting on the table.

When we got to the clinic, they got me in right away. Oliver came right into the room with me, although I hadn't asked him to. Fortunately, nobody tried to get me to change into one of those humiliating exam gowns that flap open in the back. I hadn't bothered changing out of my baggy flannel pajamas, so I was able to roll the bottoms up over my knees and expose the flesh in question.

"How did this happen?" the nurse asked. She pursed her lips and held her pen poised over the form on her clipboard.

"I ran into a cactus—slid into a cactus, to be completely accurate."

"Did you not see the cactus?" The nurse looked increasingly suspicious.

"It was dark," I said. "We were night hiking."

I pointed over at Oliver and immediately realized that I shouldn't have brought him into it. If I told the nurse the truth, that Oliver and I had been out late at night traipsing through the tumbleweeds in search of alien life forms, she'd for sure think I was lying. She was looking censoriously over at Oliver as if she suspected him of throwing me into a cactus in a fit of rage.

The nurse obviously thought she was dealing with a case of domestic violence, although I couldn't wrap my mind around the fact that she seemed to think Oliver and I were a couple. Oliver was way out of my league, clean-shaven Oliver, at any rate.

"We were stargazing," Oliver said. "There was a meteor shower last night, so we went on a night hike and had an unfortunate tangle with a barrel cactus."

"That's exactly what happened," I insisted and pointed down at my legs. "Are you going to get these spines out, or will I have to wait for the doctor?"

It took two hours, but by the time I left the clinic my legs were free of spiny plant matter, and I was finally free of pain thanks to the shot and the prescription painkillers I'd picked up at the pharmacy on the way out the door.

"I want to go out and look at where we saw the lights," I said to Oliver as we neared Little Tombstone.

"Are you sure you're up to all that walking?" Oliver protested. "We can drive part of the way, but I'm pretty sure—"

"Don't pull in at the café! Keep driving!" I yelled at Oliver.

I knew I sounded like a crazy woman, but I'd just caught sight of a figure sitting on the steps of the Bird Cage Café. It was my cousin Freida, and I was in no condition to deal with that creature from the black lagoon.

Chapter Fourteen

I considered throwing myself down on the floorboards, but I didn't think the condition of my perforated legs would allow it, so I just hunkered down in my seat. It was too little, too late. Freida was standing to her feet and looking right at me as we came up even with Little Tombstone.

"Never mind," I told Oliver. "Go ahead and pull in."

"Who is that?" he asked. "Why is she smiling at you like that?"

"That's my cousin. Second cousin, actually, and she only smiles like that when she's about to perpetrate an evil act."

"Want me to stay with you?" Oliver asked as I reached for the door handle. Freida was already approaching the car.

"No," I said. "I've never known her to be violent, although I wouldn't put it past her to manipulate some weak-minded weasel into inflicting bodily harm on somebody else."

It was as I spoke that I realized who was behind the threat note and the broken water pipe. Freida hadn't done those things—and I was not one bit closer to figuring out who had committed the actual sabotage—but I was pretty sure she'd been the one who'd put the perpetrator up to it.

"Hello, Freida," I said, pasting a smile on my face. I could feel Oliver still hovering in the background.

"Let's go upstairs," Freida said. "There's something you need to see."

"Sure, but I'll need to take Earp out first thing. I just got back from the clinic."

"The clinic?"

"I had a clash of wills with a cactus."

"Oh." Freida was looking at me like I was insane.

"I'll be fine," I said to Oliver, who was still haunting me like a shadow. What I really wanted to say was, "I appreciate your concern, but you can get lost now."

"I'll take Earp out for you," Oliver suggested, "so you don't have to navigate the stairs twice."

"That would be great," I told him and hobbled painfully up the back stairs, Freida and Oliver at my heels.

Oliver disappeared downstairs with Earp, and Freida stood in the middle of Aunt Geraldine's living room, looking around distastefully.

"This is a wreck," she said. "The whole place is falling apart."

I wanted to ask her why she wanted Little Tombstone so badly since it was in such a sorry state, but I bit my tongue.

"What is it you wanted to show me?" I said. "Oliver will be back soon with Earp."

I don't know why I felt compelled to point that out. Maybe it was because Freida was smiling more expansively than I'd ever seen her smile before, even that time she busted my grandmother's pufferfish vase and blamed me for it.

"Here." Freida thrust a folded piece of white paper into my hand. "There were a few of your grandmother's papers mixed in together with that box of love letters I took away with me last time."

I started to read the photocopied typed letter, and my knees went weak. I somehow made it to the couch, the paper still clutched in my hand. I forced myself to read all the way to the end, where I ran a shaky finger over my grandmother's handwritten signature.

I heard Oliver return with Earp. The pug ran over to me, jumped up on the couch, and stationed himself beside me, growling softly, while he kept a wary eye on Freida.

"Are you OK?" I heard Oliver ask. "You look like you are about to faint."

"She's had a shock," Freida told him. She stood to her feet, and Earp bolted for the bedroom. Freida took Earp's place on the couch beside me and whispered in my ear, "You have forty-eight hours to disclaim your inheritance, or I'm going to the police and the press with that letter."

She left me there, clutching the copy of my grandmother's letter in my hand, shaken to the core.

I heard the door close behind Freida, and then Oliver was back, kneeling down in front of me with a glass of water in his hand.

"Do I need to take you back to the clinic?" he asked. "You're not having a reaction to the medication they gave you?"

"No, no," I insisted. "But could you go down and ask Juanita to come up here just as soon as she has a minute to spare?"

It was another hour before Juanita knocked on my door. By that time, I was feeling a bit calmer. I didn't try to explain; I just asked Juanita to sit down and handed her the copy of the letter.

Juanita read the letter twice.

"This can't be true," Juanita insisted. "It must be a forgery or something."

"It looks real," I told her. "It's definitely Grandma's signature."

"Are you sure?"

"I don't want to think it's a real letter—"

"I'm afraid Freida intends to stop at nothing to get ahold of Little Tombstone," said Juanita. "And she may not be the only one.

I hate to be the bearer of bad news, but I found this taped to your door as I came in."

Juanita handed me a message which had been cut and pasted using words and letters from magazines.

LEAVE LITTLE TOMBSTONE BY TOMORROW OR IT WILL BE FIRE THIS TIME.

"You don't think Freida put this on my door?" I asked Juanita.

"I don't know," she said soberly. "I don't think it's really Freida's style. Of course, I may be assuming too much."

"Assuming too much? How?"

"You know I grew up with Abigail. We were in the same grade all the way through school."

I wasn't sure where Juanita was going with this.

"Abigail was as mean as a snake," Juanita continued. "The apple didn't fall far from the tree, but I may be mistaken in assuming that Freida is mean in exactly the same way her mother was."

"Freida always gets someone else to do her dirty work," I said. "Historically speaking."

"That's exactly how Abigail was. She'd manipulate someone else into doing something downright cruel, and then pretend she had nothing to do with it. Either that, or she'd do the dirty deed herself and then pin it on some other poor fool."

"So you think someone else is delivering the threats, but Freida's the brains behind them?"

"I do," said Juanita, "This time, I think you'd better insist that the police take these threats seriously. What do you think about sending Oliver into Santa Fe to buy more fire extinguishers? I bet the only ones around this place are the ones in the kitchen."

"I wouldn't know what to tell him to buy."

"Ask him to get the wet kind, so we can use them later as replacements in the kitchen. I'm really hoping we don't have to use them."

"Wet?"

"We have to keep the wet kind in the kitchen, in case of a grease fire. The dry kind would only spread the flames."

I made my way downstairs to find Oliver and sent him off with cash and the keys to my rental car, then I went in search of Ledbetter.

When I knocked on the door of his trailer, he took a while to answer. When he did, he looked bleary-eyed, as if he'd been sleeping.

"I suppose you heard about my tangle with a barrel cactus," I said.

He nodded. I didn't bother asking how he'd heard. I was starting to realize one couldn't keep any secret for long around Little Tombstone.

"Then I suppose you know how I came to be wandering around in the sagebrush in the middle of the night?" I asked.

"I heard you were investigating an alien sighting. Hank was very impressed."

"I don't know why he should be," I said. "We didn't make it all the way out to the lights before they disappeared. That's why I was wondering if you'd be willing to go there with me and see if there's anything out there where we sighted the lights. I sent Oliver to town on an urgent errand."

"Sure," said Ledbetter. "But are you sure you're up to it?"

I wasn't sure I was up to it. My legs were hurting less, but the painkillers combined with the shock of reading my Grandmother's letter had me feeling light-headed.

I'd sent Oliver off with my rental car, and I didn't think my injured legs were up to a ride on the back of Ledbetter's motorcycle.

"Can you drive Aunt Geraldine's truck?" I asked Ledbetter.

"Sure," he said as if it were no big deal.

I held up the bristling ring of keys my aunt had left me.

"Would you happen to know which key it is?"

"I'm sure the key is in the truck," Ledbetter said. "She never bothered taking it out."

"Did you ever hear any rumors going around about hidden gold from a stagecoach holdup back in the 1800s?" I asked Ledbetter as I hobbled beside him toward my aunt's old Chevy parked around the end of the old motel.

"Yeah. I heard those stories. People have been searching for years, but nobody ever found it. If you ask me, those lights—"

We'd reached the pickup, and Ledbetter had swung open the heavy passenger side door for me. He held out his hand to help me up, but I was too busy examining what was in the bed of the pickup to acknowledge him.

"What is that?" I asked, pointing to a long, thick semi-rusted rod that was slightly pointed on both ends.

"It looks like an old axel."

Accompanying the axel was a propane torch and an old hack saw.

"You know what we're looking at?" I asked Ledbetter.

He shook his head.

"I think these are the things whoever bashed holes in the water pipes left behind."

Ledbetter hefted the axel and banged it down speculatively on the ground. It sunk in a few inches. When he pulled it out, a round hole about an inch in diameter was left behind.

"I suppose somebody could have knocked holes in the pipe this way," he said. "But it would have taken them a while."

"You know what I think?"

"What do you think?"

"This has to have been an inside job," I told Ledbetter.

Chapter Fifteen

"What do you mean about this being an 'inside job'?" Ledbetter asked as we bumped along the road up toward the location where Oliver and I had spotted the lights the night before.

"Think about it," I said. "Whoever threw that rock through my window did it while I was eating supper. They must have been hanging around waiting for me to leave the apartment. The pipes were tampered with during the early afternoon. I went out back around noon, and nothing was amiss, then I lay down on the couch for a nap and was awakened shortly after three by Oliver and Juanita telling me there was a geyser erupting in the trailer court."

"I don't follow," said Ledbetter.

"A stranger would be worried about being recognized as an intruder," I explained. "But whoever is doing these things is more comfortable working in broad daylight. He, or she, isn't worried about being recognized as being out of place."

"I guess," said Ledbetter, "but he still might get caught."

"Or she."

"Sure, I suppose."

"I got another threat note," I said.

"When?"

"Just a few minutes ago."

"What did it say?"

"It's threatening fire this time."

I saw Ledbetter's hands tense on the steering wheel, and I expected him to say something more about the note, but instead, he pulled off the side of the road.

"If we go any farther," he said, "we'll be onto Nancy Flynn's land, and she's hard on trespassers."

"Hard on them?"

"She comes after them with a shotgun."

"We aren't trespassers," I pointed out. "We're neighbors."

"It will be hard to explain that to her if she's already shot you," Ledbetter said with a perfectly straight face. I couldn't decide if he was joking or not. "Nancy keeps a shotgun on a rack in her truck, and she's always carrying. I bet she sleeps with a handgun under her pillow."

I bet Ledbetter did too, but I didn't have the nerve to ask.

I slid painfully out of the passenger seat and down to the ground. I stood for a minute on the roadside surveying the landscape.

"I think the arroyo I fell into is over there," I said, pointing to the east. "The lights were over there." I pointed to the west. "Just beyond that little rise, I think."

"You lead the way," said Ledbetter, and we headed off into the sagebrush.

It was much easier going in the daylight, despite my injuries, and it wasn't long before we came to the spot where I thought Oliver and I had seen the lights.

"Do you think we're still on Little Tombstone land out here?" I asked Ledbetter.

"I think so," he said.

There had undoubtedly been human activity in the area, either that or Hank was right about the aliens. The ground was scarred, and a wide swath of sagebrush and cactus had been removed.

"Do those look like backhoe tracks to you?" I asked Ledbetter.

"Yes, and at least one truck. There's been a lot of traffic in and out of here."

"I wonder if all these vehicles have been coming in from the road."

"There's only one way to find out," said Ledbetter.

We made our way back to the pickup, and Ledbetter drove slowly along the road. We crept past the old cemetery on the hill. As we passed, I could see the erosion that Morticia had talked about. We continued keeping an eagle eye out for tracks leading off the gravel road while we rounded the back of the hill, but we soon reached a locked gate with a sign that warned us that trespassers would be shot on sight.

"This is Nancy Flynn's ranch?"

"Yep."

"So whoever is digging on Little Tombstone land has to be coming across her land."

"Looks like it."

There was nothing to do but turn around.

"What were you about to say earlier?" I asked Ledbetter. "Right before we found that stuff in the back of the pickup? It sounded like you had some theory about the lights."

"I was just going to suggest that somebody might be on the hunt for that gold again."

It was a plausible theory. More plausible than Hank's supposition that we were being invaded by alien life forms.

When we got back to Little Tombstone, Oliver was back with the fire extinguishers.

I hid one in the utility closet under the stairs. I gave one each to Ledbetter and Oliver and charged them with guarding the extinguishers with their lives. Then I took one over to Hank. The door to the Curio Shop was locked, and a Closed sign hung on the door to the museum. I left the extinguisher on the step with a note taped to it. I took the single remaining extinguisher and concealed it under the kitchen sink in my aunt's apartment.

Juanita and I inspected the older extinguishers in the café. They all seemed to be in working order. I had done all I could. There was nothing to do but wait for the saboteur to make his or her next move.

Around ten the following morning, just as I sat down to a plate of migas in the café dining room, I smelled smoke.

"Do you smell that?" I asked Chamomile, who was restocking the napkin dispensers before going on her morning break.

Chamomile disappeared into the kitchen. Almost immediately, I heard her scream, then she came running out of the kitchen yelling for help.

I rushed into the kitchen to find Juanita battling a grease fire, or rather Juanita attempting to battle a grease fire. She was sorely deficient in ammunition.

Juanita was standing in front of a fry vat that had erupted in flames, trying to discharge the special wet-fire extinguisher she kept nearby for just such an unlucky occasion, but the extinguisher appeared to be jammed.

"Turn off the propane!" Juanita yelled. I didn't know where the shut-off for the propane was, but Chamomile materialized from somewhere behind me and darted over to the wall and turned a valve.

It did nothing to extinguish the fire because the grease was still burning, but at least we weren't about to go up with a bang, providing Chamomile knew what she was doing.

I went to the closet under the stairs and brought out the extinguisher I'd wrapped in rags and tucked behind a case of paper towels.

I thrust the new extinguisher into Juanita's hands, and she discharged its entire contents into the column of flames coming up from the deep fat fryer.

By the time Marco wandered in from the dish room, and Oliver materialized from the front porch where he'd been putting the finishing touches on the broken step, it was all over.

"What happened?" Oliver asked.

"Grease fire," Juanita said. "I don't understand how it happened. It was probably caused by a thermostat malfunction, but I hadn't even turned that fry vat on."

"The note!" I said, "The threat note promising a fire if I don't leave Little Tombstone: this was it."

"I certainly hope this was it," said Juanita, "because we're down at least two fire extinguishers."

Chapter Sixteen

We stood around soberly, looking at the smoke-blackened ceiling above the fry vat until Marco announced that he had to finish the dishes. Chamomile excused herself to finish tidying the dining room, and Oliver went back to working on the steps.

I remained standing beside Juanita, staring at the mess.

"What if someone ends up getting hurt?" I said. "The broken water pipe was a pain, but it put no one in danger. This is different—somebody could have died. You could have gotten severely burned if you hadn't known how to put it out. We could have all gone up in a flash of propane if the fire had spread too far."

"It wasn't that serious." Juanita tried to sound reassuring but missed by a mile. It's hard to sound really reassuring when your voice is trembling.

"I'll call the police," I said.

It's funny how once you've had dead bodies discovered on your property—never mind they've probably been dead for decades—the police become extremely attentive to your concerns.

Officer Reyes showed up in less than an hour to take photographs of our blackened ceiling.

"You're very lucky it wasn't worse," he told Juanita and me. "You've already confirmed with all your staff that no one accidentally turned on the fryer and forgot about it?"

"I only have two people who work for me," Juanita told the officer. "My waitress, Chamomile, helps out in the kitchen when things are slow in the dining room, but she swears she hasn't touched the fry vat in days. My dishwasher, Marco, rarely comes into the kitchen at all. He'd have no reason to touch it.

"Are you sure it couldn't have been turned on by accident? Couldn't someone have inadvertently bumped the knobs?" Officer Reyes asked Juanita. "Is it possible that you turned it on yourself and then forgot about it?"

"It has to be lit by hand with an open flame," Juanita said frostily. She looked like she wanted to sock the officer. She'd reached the age where people start to get sensitive about anyone more than twenty years younger than they are questioning their memory. "The fryer isn't something that could get turned on by accident," Juanita told Officer Reyes. "Even if it had somehow been on for hours, that doesn't begin to explain why it suddenly went up in flames."

"What do you think might have happened?" Officer Reyes asked.

"Fires like this one are sometimes caused by a thermostat malfunctioning so that the oil gets too hot and eventually combusts, but that's very rare," Juanita told Officer Reyes. "I've worked in restaurants for almost fifty years, and I've only known a fryer to spontaneously catch on fire once."

"There's something else that strongly suggests this could be arson," I told Officer Reyes. "Look at these."

I handed the officer the two threat notes I'd received.

"I reported the first note to the Sheriff's office already," I told him. "But the second one threatening me with fire was discovered yesterday taped to the door of the apartment I'm staying in."

The officer had me drop the cut-and-pasted note into an evidence bag and said he'd take it back to the station with him. He told Juanita not to touch the fryer. Someone would come to take it away and send it off to determine if the thermostat had been tampered with.

"If the thermostat has been messed with," Juanita told me after Officer Reyes had departed, "not just anyone would know how to do that."

"No, they wouldn't," I agreed, "but we live in the age of the internet, and a smart, resourceful person can find detailed instructions about how to do almost anything on the web."

"I wonder what's next," Juanita said wearily. "Once whoever is behind the flood and the fire finds out you won't be driven away, what will they resort to after that?"

It didn't take long for the next threat to be delivered.

I'd spent the morning dealing with the aftermath of the fire, and Earp was sure to be upstairs agitating to be let out. Before I went up, I went in search of Oliver, who'd requested the use of my rental car to drive into Santa Fe after more building supplies.

My Australian hitchhiker was making remarkable progress on the lengthy list of tasks I'd given him. I was going to have to start paying him. Three meals a day and a spot on the floor to roll out his sleeping bag were not adequate compensation for his accomplishments.

I gave Oliver the keys and the last of my cash. I was going to have to visit the ATM again soon. I had a myriad things to do to put my affairs in order, what with my impending divorce and my new status as proprietress of Little Tombstone, but I was having trouble accomplishing much between dealing with paranoid tenants and periodic sabotage.

I had just put Earp's leash on and was heading downstairs again when Oliver met me on the stairs. He didn't say anything, just held out a piece of bright pink poster board which said in big block letters: PREPARE FOR PESTILENCE.

"It was shoved under your windscreen," Oliver told me after I'd turned the placard over and discovered nothing more on the other side. "What does pestilence mean?"

"Not sure," I told Oliver. "It sounds biblical. I'll go next door and ask Pastor Freddy."

"I thought next door was a barbershop."

"It is a barbershop, but it also functions as an informal house of worship on Sundays."

I let Earp do his business, then took him with me to Freddy Fernandez's barbershop. I went alone. There was too much to do, so I'd sent Oliver on to Santa Fe for supplies, despite the impending arrival of pestilence, whatever that might be.

A bell jingled over the door as I entered the barbershop. There was a man in the barber chair who I recognized as Jimmy, the backhoe guy. Jimmy had a bib around his neck. His head was thrown back, and he was snoring. Jimmy's hair was neatly trimmed, so I presumed that Freddy, the devout barber, must be somewhere close by.

I decided to wait. I tethered Earp's leash to one of the two chairs provided for waiting customers and sat down in the other. Earp flopped down at my feet and lay there until a fly circling his head got him so irritated that he snapped at it. When the fly got away, Earp gave a sharp bark, which woke Jimmy up mid-snore. The excavator shook himself a little like he'd forgotten where he was.

"Oh, hello, Emma," he said jovially when he'd pulled himself together and wiped the drool from his cheek with the cuff of his shirt. "Here for a haircut?"

"No, I have a theological question for Pastor Freddy."

"You know," Jimmy said, lowering his voice, "Freddy's not really a pastor."

Chapter Seventeen

I told Jimmy that I was fully aware that Freddy Fernandez was not a licensed minister of the gospel. I merely sought his Bible knowledge, not someone to marry or bury me. It was when I said the word bury that I thought of earthmoving and realized this was an ideal opportunity to quiz Jimmy about the disturbed earth on the Little Tombstone property that adjoined his sister-in-law's ranch.

"There's something I'm wondering about," I prefaced my interrogation. "I happened to be out behind the trailer court at Little Tombstone and noticed that somebody had been digging out there. Did my Aunt Geraldine happen to hire you to do any earth-moving for her?"

I watched Jimmy carefully, but he didn't flinch. Of course, just because someone had been running a backhoe behind the trailer court, it didn't mean that person had to be Jimmy. Nevertheless, since the equipment had almost certainly been brought across the property line between Nancy Flynn's ranch and Little Tombstone, Jimmy seemed the most likely suspect.

"No, Nancy has me do a little work for her every once in a while, but it's all been up by the barns."

"I haven't gotten a bill yet for all that work you did getting our water back on," I said.

"Don't worry about it," said Jimmy. "Just a neighborly act. I was happy to do it."

Of course, after he said that, it would have seemed churlish of me to harp on about the unauthorized earth-moving, so I let the subject drop.

Soon after, Freddy came back. Jimmy paid his bill, and I had the barbershop and Pastor Freddy all to myself.

"You want a haircut?" Freddy asked.

"No, I just have a quick question. Juanita tells me you're quite a Bible scholar. Can you explain where the phrase 'Flood, Fire, and Pestilence' comes from?"

"I don't know if that exact phrase appears anywhere in the Bible," Freddy said, "but it sounds sort of like the last three of the four horsemen of the apocalypse: war, famine, and pestilence."

"What is pestilence?"

"Like an epidemic, but sometimes people use it to mean a plague. Like the plagues in the book of Exodus."

"Or plague as in the medieval disease?"

Freddy said he didn't know. He wasn't an expert on medieval history.

"Someone is threatening us," I told Freddy. "So far, they've threatened flood and broken one of our water pipes. Then they threatened fire, and the deep fat fryer in the café inexplicably erupted in flames. You've probably heard all about it already from Marco."

"I came over to look the day the pipe broke. I saw they were digging up a bunch of old bones. Any idea yet who was buried under there?"

I told Freddy there'd been no new developments in identifying the skeletons. He expressed hope that the poor souls would be identified soon for the sake of their surviving loved ones.

"Now, the same person who busted up the water pipe and started the fry vat on fire is threatening to visit pestilence upon us," I told Freddy. "What do you suppose they intend to do this time?"

"I guess it depends upon what **they** think pestilence means. What do you think the word pestilence means?"

Freddy was not asking me the question. Instead, he directed it to his son, Marco, who came into the shop from the room in the back. I wondered if the whole family lived over the barbershop, or if they had a home elsewhere. Maybe Marco was simply coming in to say hi to his father during his afternoon break.

"Pestilence?" Marco echoed. "You mean like swarms of frogs and bugs and stuff? Like in the book of Exodus?"

Freddy didn't bother to correct his son, but Pastor Freddy had made his point. That threat of "pestilence" could mean we were in for just about anything.

"You guys live here?" I asked as I stood to leave.

I looked at Marco as I asked the question, but he was looking at the floor. I had yet to see the boy make direct eye contact with another living soul. I wondered if when he stood in front of a mirror, he looked even himself in the eye.

"Upstairs," Freddy said, pointing up at the ceiling. "It's just me and Marco since his mother moved back to Albuquerque."

The rest of the day was uneventful. There were no outbreaks of dread diseases; we were not overrun with rats or frogs, nor did a swarm of locusts appear.

By evening, I had relaxed a little. I decided to finish going through the box of scrapbooks and albums where I'd found the articles about the stagecoach robbery and the probable treasure map. I'd tucked those away between the mattress and box springs in Aunt Geraldine's bedroom.

I took the remainder of the scrapbooks down from where I'd stashed them in the tumble dryer in case Freida came back for more stuff. I was happy to pass them on to my cousins eventually,

113

but not until I'd sifted through them for clues as to what my Aunt Geraldine had been up to all these years.

The first few albums I looked at were entertaining, but not particularly illuminating. There were pictures of Christmases and birthdays and family vacations. They all featured a little girl, and later a teenager, who was unmistakably my cousin Abigail. There were lots of pictures of her up until Christmas 1979, and then abruptly, for a few years at least, Aunt Geraldine and Uncle Ricky had taken to celebrating holidays without her.

Abigail's absence coincided roughly with her pregnancy. I decided that must have been the reason my cousin had stopped showing up in photos for a few years. Perhaps, Abigail had moved away for a while. It had been a different era. Maybe being a teenaged unwed mother had been such a big deal she'd gone off somewhere and not returned to Amatista until the twins were a few years old. I made a mental note to ask Juanita about it and moved on to the next item, a manila envelope of newspaper clippings.

All the clippings concerned a couple who'd gone missing sometime around the first of the year in 1980. The clippings followed the trajectory of the investigation. The couple, Greg and Stacy Halverson, had been reported missing mid-January. By the end of January, their considerably damaged vehicle, a green 1967 Plymouth Fury, had been discovered dumped into an arroyo just off a remote road a mile or so south of Amatista.

There were numerous subsequent clippings that followed developments in the investigation. Several suspects had been questioned and then cleared. Possible sightings of the couple had been reported, but these were never substantiated, and the Halversons' bodies never turned up. The time between new stories became increasingly long, and the clipping at the very bottom of the pile, which simply reported that there was nothing new to report, was dated two years after the date of the Halversons' disappearance. There were a few handwritten notations on the clippings, but it didn't look like Aunt Geraldine's handwriting.

I took the manila envelope of clippings and the album from my cousin Abigail's childhood and stashed them under the mattress with the treasure map and the scrapbook about the stagecoach robbery.

While I was adjusting the mattress back into position over the box springs, Earp came in and nosed around my ankles. As he tried to wriggle in between me and the bed, he rubbed against my injured legs, and I stumbled backward in pain.

That's how I knocked over the nightstand.

It was a mess. The nightstand went over, spilling out the contents of both the small drawer and the lower open shelf. The lamp on top of the nightstand toppled, and the shade broke. The water glass I kept next to the bed fell over and drenched the lot.

I picked up the protesting Earp, hobbled to the bathroom, and locked him in.

It was not until I'd picked up the nightstand and was putting everything back in place that I realized something was very wrong.

Uncle Ricky's antique pearl-handled revolver which had been tucked behind the paperbacks in the bottom shelf of the nightstand had gone missing, case and all.

Chapter Eighteen

It took me eons to fall asleep that night. I hadn't had a really good night's sleep since my return to Little Tombstone, but that night was especially fitful. Somewhere, out there in the darkness, somebody had my Uncle Ricky's revolver, and that same someone had rifled through the apartment when I wasn't looking. That meant that someone either had a key or was adept at picking locks.

I felt relatively secure with the deadbolt engaged, but there was nothing I could do to keep someone with a key (or burglars' tools) out of the apartment whenever I left it.

The first thing the next morning, I went looking for Oliver. He was under the sink in the café ladies' room, trying to find the source of a slow leak in the drainpipe. When I called his name, he hastily withdrew his head from under the sink.

"If you stay on long enough," I told him, "this place might get worked back into shape."

I was joking, of course. Eliminating the drips in drainpipes was all well and good, but the entire place needed a new roof, and acres of peeling paint would need removal before any competent painter would consider adding a fresh coat.

"There's something more urgent," I told Oliver as I handed him the keys to the rental car and the one remaining valid credit card to my name.

I'd run out of cash, and it was probably naïve of me to hand off my credit card to a complete stranger, but that's just how I am. When I trust someone, I act like it. When I don't trust someone, I take prompt action to protect myself. That's why I was so set on getting the locks changed on every building at Little Tombstone as soon as possible.

"Rekey everything," I told Oliver. "If it can't be rekeyed, then install a whole new lock. Don't let the new keys out of your sight for a second. Key every building differently. I don't want a master made. Guard those with your life until—"

I was cut short by the arrival of Hank. He staggered through the front door of the Bird Cage Café and made it halfway across the dining room before he collapsed on the floor.

"What's wrong? Hank? Hank!" I said as I bent over the unresponsive old man. I took my phone out of my pocket and handed it up to Oliver. "Call 911 and tell them to send an ambulance."

Hank's face was swollen almost beyond recognition, and his hands and neck were covered with welts. I felt his pulse. It was weak and fluttering, but he was alive.

"Bees," Oliver said, as he waited on the line with the emergency services operator who'd informed us that an ambulance had been dispatched, but that it would be at least twenty minutes before help arrived. "I'm pretty sure Hank's gotten into a nest of bees. That happened to a mate of mine when we were kids. He decided to harass a hive of bees, and they came out at him with a vengeance."

"If it is bees, in twenty minutes, Hank could be dead," I said. "Stay with him, and I'll see if someone has an EpiPen."

Juanita and Chamomile were already hovering over us. Marco was hanging around the dish room door, trying to look cool and disinterested but failing by a mile. For the first time since I'd met him, he had an actual expression on his face. He looked genuinely worried. Maybe there was some good in the boy, after all. No one present carried an epinephrine injector, so I ran out back to check with Morticia and Ledbetter.

Apparently, Hank's days on earth were not yet numbered, because when I banged frantically on Morticia's door, she opened up right away. I told her Hank had been badly stung by bees and did she have an EpiPen. She didn't, but the woman whose fortune she'd been telling was a nurse and carried one with her. The nurse rushed to the café dining room and administered the dose of epinephrine. By the time the ambulance arrived, Hank was coming around.

They took him into the hospital in Santa Fe. I expected Hank to refuse treatment, now that he was conscious again, and his swelling had started going down, but, apparently, his objections to "Big Pharma" and the "Medical Industrial Complex" were considerably muted by having just been pulled back from the brink of death.

"How in the world did he get into a beehive?" I wondered aloud after the ambulance had taken him off to the hospital.

Hank had turned down my offer to accompany him, although he had given me a phone number and instructed me to call a lady friend of his named Phyllis. The existence of a lady friend in Hank's life probably explained why he spent the night out on occasion. I was terribly curious to meet this Phyllis person. I couldn't imagine what kind of woman would fall for Hank.

"Hank doesn't seem to spend much time outside," Oliver said. "Do you suppose that bees got into the Curio Shop somehow?"

"The pestilence!" I said it so loudly that it made Oliver jump. "The bees must be the promised pestilence."

"Well, if those bees attacked Hank, then they'll attack someone else if they aren't taken care of," said Oliver. "We'd better figure out where Hank got into them."

We started our search for the bees' nest next door at the Curio Shop and the Museum of the Unexplained. As soon as I reached for the swinging screen door which hung on the outside of the entrance to the Curio Shop, I knew we'd found what we'd been looking for.

Several bees were drunkenly darting around the entrance. Through the screen door, I could see that the solid interior door was flung open—probably by Hank in his haste to get away— giving me a clear view inside the Curio Shop. The place was swarming with bees.

"I think this is a job for a professional beekeeper or an exterminator," I said to Oliver. "We'd better put up a warning sign for people to keep out. Stand back in the street, and I'll just open the screen door long enough to close the solid door inside. That should keep the bees contained until the cavalry arrives."

I got stung twice for my efforts, but I managed to close and lock the door to the shop. I had to search for ten minutes through my ring of keys to find the one that fit the entrance to the Museum of the Unexplained, but twenty minutes after the ambulance had taken Hank away, the perimeter was secured, and an exterminator was on his way.

I belatedly sent Oliver off to remove the locksets on everything but the building containing the bees so he could have them rekeyed in Santa Fe. I hoped nothing horrible would happen while he was away, but so far, the mischief-maker around Little Tombstone hadn't made a move without a warning first.

Thinking of warnings brought my mind back to the ultimatum issued by my cousin Freida.

If I didn't relinquish my inheritance, Freida had threatened to take my grandmother's confession letter to the police and to the press. According to Freida, I had less than twenty-four more hours to figure out what to do.

I decided that I needed some good legal advice. Although Mr. Wendell had declined to get involved in my defense against Freida and Georgia's contest to my Great Aunt Geraldine's will, I had a feeling that all the skullduggery going around Little Tombstone might pique his interest enough to get him to change his mind.

I didn't call ahead. Oliver had my rental car, so I set out on foot through downtown Amatista toward Mr. Wendell's office on the south edge of the village.

When I got to Mr. Wendell's office, there was someone with him. The door to the inner office was shut, and I could hear the indistinct murmur of voices. There was a desk for a secretary, but I had yet to see anyone sitting at it, which made me wonder if it might be just for show. Maybe Mr. Wendell had not yet found a suitable underling among the inhabitants of Amatista. I imagined Mr. Wendell might have quite a challenge finding a local receptionist-type who would be compatible with the ambiance of his office space.

I waited a full fifteen minutes before the door opened, and Nancy Flynn came out.

"Mrs. Iverson!" Mr. Wendell seemed surprised to see me, but he quickly returned to equilibrium. "I'm glad you stopped by," he continued more calmly. "Miss Flynn has something she'd like to discuss with you."

Chapter Nineteen

Nancy Flynn stood in the middle of Mr. Wendell's waiting room, shifting her weight from one cowboy-booted foot to the other. Mr. Wendell might be glad I'd stopped by, but my neighbor clearly wasn't.

"This is very awkward," she began. "That's why I wanted to involve a lawyer."

"What's awkward?" I asked.

"You'd better come in, and I'll explain," Mr. Wendell said and escorted Nancy and me back inside his office.

Mr. Wendell sat behind his desk. Nancy and I each took one of the slick leather chairs Mr. Wendell kept for the use of his clients.

"There's something your great aunt neglected to inform me about," Mr. Wendell began. "It's probable she did not inform me of it because she was unaware of it herself."

This left me as much in the dark as ever, but when Mr. Wendell handed me the papers he held in his hand, it all became clearer.

I read through the document, examined the map, and read through the document again a second time. Omitting all the legalese, it seemed that my Great Uncle Ricky had signed off on a boundary line adjustment over thirty years ago. For reasons unknown, to me at least, he'd given Nancy Flynn a roughly nine-acre parcel that adjoined her ranch. I looked at the map for a third time.

"These nine acres which were transferred over to you," I addressed Nancy. "Is that the piece of vacant land between the back fence of the trailer court and your ranch?"

Nancy Flynn nodded.

"Did Aunt Geraldine know about this?"

"No," said Nancy. "Richard and I—"

"You had an affair?" I could hear my voice rising. "Did Aunt Geraldine know?"

"She didn't know," Nancy said, tacitly acknowledging the existence of the affair. "She didn't know a lot of things. Richard signed that land over to me because I'd loaned him a large sum of money, which he could not repay. He'd maxed out several lines of credits your aunt had no idea he'd opened. Richard was expecting a windfall which never materialized."

The windfall Uncle Ricky must have been counting on was finding the gold cache from the stagecoach robbery. If Aunt Geraldine's treasure map could be believed, Uncle Ricky had come very close to finding it; he'd just died a little too soon.

I wondered if Uncle Ricky had ever had any intention of letting Aunt Geraldine in on his little secret, had he succeeded in finding the treasure. I wondered if he'd planned to hide his discovery from Aunt Geraldine and share his windfall with Nancy instead.

"Is this all legal?" I asked Mr. Wendell. "I mean, was Uncle Ricky within his rights to just sign over the land like that?"

"I already looked into the legality of the boundary line adjustment on Miss Flynn's behalf," Mr. Wendell said. "During the period of time when the transfer of land was recorded, the entire acreage on which Little Tombstone sits was solely in the names of a Betty Wright—your grandmother, I presume—and

124

Richard Montgomery. Mrs. Wright also signed off on the adjustment to the boundary line, so—"

"My grandmother knew?" I turned to Nancy.

Nancy nodded. Her already reddened face was even redder than usual. She was clearly ashamed of herself, but not so ashamed that she was willing to let the land go.

"Am I right in assuming that you haven't exercised your rights to the land before out of respect for my aunt?" I asked Nancy.

"I didn't want her to know," Nancy said.

Apparently, neither did my grandmother.

"Well," I said, "It all looks legal enough, and I do understand why it didn't come up earlier, so I'll just think of it as becoming even closer neighbors than we already were."

Nancy looked like she could have hugged me, but she restrained herself. That nine acres seemed to mean an awful lot to her considering she already owned a thousand acres or so of sagebrush already.

"By the way," I said, as Nancy stood up to leave. "I know now that it's your land and has been for some time, but are you planning on putting up a new barn or something out there?"

All the relief drained out of Nancy's face.

"No," she said. "I'm not planning on building anything on it."

"That's funny. I could have sworn that someone was clearing a building site out behind the trailer court. I happened to be wandering around out there, and it looks like someone has moved quite a lot of dirt."

"Oh, that's just where my nephews like to ride their dirt bikes," she said. "I didn't think they were doing any harm."

"It didn't look like dirt bike tracks," I insisted. "It looked a lot more like someone had been digging holes with a backhoe and then filling them in again."

"I'm sure no one's been digging," Nancy insisted.

"Well, I must have been wrong," I said. "Hank Edwards is convinced we're in the middle of an alien invasion because of the lights he keeps seeing out there in the wee hours of the morning, but if your nephews like tearing around on their dirt bikes at two AM, more power to them."

Nancy stared at me with her mouth open, then regained her composure sufficiently to thank Mr. Wendell for his time.

"Tell your nephews to watch out for barrel cactuses," I said to her retreating back. "The spines hurt like the dickens to get out once they're in."

"You took that well," said Mr. Wendell as soon as the front door of the building had closed behind Nancy.

"It's a believable story," I told him. "I always suspected that my Uncle Ricky wasn't the most loyal of men, and he was never good with money if all the stories my grandmother told me were accurate. I do have reason to believe Uncle Ricky might have been expecting a windfall. Nancy Flynn's explanation of the boundary-line adjustment rings true. I'm just not completely convinced that all that disturbed dirt out there is the result of a couple of boys on dirt bikes."

Mr. Wendell sat across his desk from me and laced and unlaced his fingers, a trifle nervously, I thought. The man had an impeccable manicure.

"What can I do for you?" Mr. Wendell finally asked.

I hastily produced the copy of the possibly-or-possibly-not-genuine letter from my grandmother, then folded my hands in my lap to hide my chipped polish and ragged cuticles.

"I assume you've heard about the discovery of the bodies under the trailer court at Little Tombstone?" I said.

I couldn't imagine that Mr. Wendell had not. It had even made the local news. Although I'd declined to be interviewed, Jimmy had been happy to take my place in the limelight. I thought he'd rather exaggerated his role in the discovery, but that was fine with me. I didn't particularly care to become a local celebrity because I'd discovered a pile of old bones.

Besides, if anyone deserved credit for the discovery, it was Earp. Earp had known there were bodies buried down there long before the rest of us had a clue.

"I did hear that a couple of skeletons were dug up," Mr. Wendell said. "I understand they were unearthed during some routine repairs to the water main."

"I would not characterize them as routine repairs," I said. "It was clearly a case of sabotage."

Chapter Twenty

"Sabotage?" Mr. Wendell said.

Clearly, he'd not heard the news that someone—my money was on Freida being the mastermind—was trying to force me out of Little Tombstone.

"I've gotten a series of anonymous threats. First, it was a threat of flood; then somebody busted up the water main. Then it was a threat of fire, and the fry vat in the café malfunctioned. That nearly sent the whole place up in flames. Finally, yesterday, I got a note threatening me with 'pestilence.' I wasn't even sure what pestilence was, but this morning, whoever was behind the notes made good on their threat by planting a hive of angry bees in the Curio Shop. Poor Hank got severely stung. He could have died if Morticia hadn't happened to have been giving a reading to a client who carried an EpiPen on her."

Mr. Wendell stared at me, wide-eyed. It seemed he hadn't heard that the sleepy village of Amatista was fast transforming into a hotbed of crime. He shook his head a couple of times and then transferred his attention to the copy of the letter from my grandmother I'd slid across the desk to him.

"The letter is purported to be written by my grandmother," I told Mr. Wendell.

"Betty Wright?"

"It's typed, but the signature looks genuine," I told him. "I just can't believe my Grandmother would be confessing to anything like that."

"Sometimes, in life, one has to become comfortable with ambiguity," Mr. Wendell said.

"I don't have that luxury," I told him. "Freida is blackmailing me with that letter. She says that if I don't sign over Little Tombstone to her by this time tomorrow, then she's going to go to the police and the press with this letter."

"But your grandmother has been dead for years," Mr. Wendell pointed out. "Does it really matter what Freida does with the letter?"

"My grandmother may have passed away, but Freida knows how much I loved her. I couldn't bear for people to think my grandmother had done something so horrible. Betty Wright was a pillar of the community for decades. There isn't a person in the entire town of Amatista who has a bad word to say about her. I can't allow their memories of her to be ruined like that."

"But the letter claims that it was an accident."

"I know, but the letter also claims my grandmother was under the influence, not to mention the lengths she supposedly went to in order to conceal her involvement in the deaths."

"Did your grandmother have a problem with alcohol?"

"No!" I was talking much too loudly, but I couldn't contain my indignation. "My grandmother had a glass of wine on Christmas and Easter and possibly champagne at New Year's. My cousin Abigail is the only person in our family who's ever had a drinking problem."

"Abigail? You mean Mrs. Montgomery's daughter."

"Yes, Freida and Georgia's mother. She's been very quiet throughout this whole thing. I haven't heard boo from her since my Great Aunt Geraldine died."

"Perhaps, you should pay her a visit," Mr. Wendell suggested. "Since she hasn't yet expressed any intention of contesting the will, there might be something she knows that your cousins aren't telling you."

I decided this was good advice and fully intended to take it, only I didn't have a chance to head up to Santa Fe to pay Abigail a visit because, by the time I got back to Little Tombstone, things had taken a very sinister turn.

As I walked along Highway 14, which did double duty as Amatista's Main Street, a police car tore past me, lights flashing, and screeched to a stop in front of the Bird Cage Café.

I went up the steps into the Café and looked around, but the place was deserted. I called out for Juanita, then Chamomile, and finally for Oliver, but no one answered.

I walked to the back entrance and found that the door had been left open. I stepped out into the alley behind the café and followed the sound of voices to the trailer court.

There was quite a congregation clustered around the open door of room one of the motel. Of all the residents and employees of Little Tombstone, only Hank and Marco were missing.

As I approached the group surrounding the open door of the derelict motel room, Officer Reyes came out, a very grim look on his face.

"The ambulance is coming," he said, "but I'm afraid it's too late."

"What's going on?" I asked.

Officer Reyes looked at me as if he didn't want to say. Morticia came over and put one arm around me before she said, "I'm sorry, but it looks like your cousin Freida may have shot herself."

"Shot herself?"

That didn't sound like Freida at all. If Morticia had told me Freida had shot someone else, then I wouldn't have had nearly so much trouble wrapping my mind around it.

"Who found her?" I asked no one in particular.

"Oliver did," Morticia said.

I looked over at Oliver. He was looking very pale and shaken.

"I heard a couple of shots," Oliver told me. "I was on the other side of the motel, installing one of the locks that I got rekeyed this morning when I heard them. When I came around the front to see what was happening, the motel room door was hanging open, and she was just lying there—"

Officer Reyes had instructed us to stay out of the motel room while he went back to his car for a roll of tape to block off access to the scene, but I scuttled up to the door and looked inside.

We might have been instructed to stay out of room one, but Officer Reyes had not said anything about not taking a peek through the door.

As soon as I saw Freida, I wished that I hadn't let my curiosity get the better of me.

My cousin lay sprawled out on an old box spring, with a single bullet hole in the center of her forehead. She was clutching an antique pearl-handled revolver in her left hand.

Chapter Twenty-One

The ambulance came and took Freida's body away, and a swarm of police cars parked out front of the motel. Juanita put up a Closed sign in the window of the Bird Cage Café and sent Chamomile home for the evening.

"Where was Marco during all the commotion?" I asked Juanita. "I didn't see him out back after the police came."

"I'd sent him home," Juanita told me. "He was sick again. I found him throwing up in the dirt back by the dumpster. The poor thing must have a terrible case of the flu. He looked like he was about to pass out."

"When did you find Marco throwing up?"

"Right before Oliver came in and told us Freida had shot herself."

"So, you didn't hear the gunshots?"

"No. We don't hear much back in the kitchen. I like to have the radio on, and it can get pretty noisy banging pots and pans around."

"You know," I said as I looked around to make sure no one else was in earshot. "I don't think Freida shot herself."

"Why?"

"I looked in before they took her away, and the gun was in her left hand. Freida is right-handed. Somebody else fired the shot and then placed the gun in her hand."

"Are you sure you weren't confused?" Juanita asked. "It had to have been distressing to see her like that. I couldn't bring myself to look inside."

"I'm positive someone shot Freida, and whoever killed her must have been a virtual stranger, or they wouldn't have made such an obvious mistake."

"Do the police think it's a simple case of suicide?"

"I don't know."

"Poor Freida," said Juanita.

She seemed a lot fonder of Freida now that she was dead. I had to admit that I was feeling quite a bit more pity for my cruel cousin than I'd ever felt before.

"There's something else," I told Juanita. "You remember that old pearl-handled revolver that used be Uncle Ricky's? Until yesterday it lived in the back of the nightstand beside Aunt Geraldine's bed. I'm sure that's the gun Freida had in her hand."

"You mean that antique gun with the shiny handle?" Juanita asked. "Your Uncle Ricky used to take that out back and shoot at tin cans, but half the time it refused to fire."

"That's the one, and I'd bet anything it's got my fingerprints all over it."

The very next day, I was politely but firmly requested to make an appearance at the county sheriff's office.

I took a seat at a table in what looked like a breakroom while Officer Reyes sat across from me. He took great pains to inform me that I was there voluntarily, and that I was not a suspect. I'd have been a lot less nervous if he hadn't felt the need to be quite so adamant about how nobody was accusing me of being responsible for my cousin Freida's death.

"I don't believe it was a suicide," I told Officer Reyes after he'd taken my statement about where I'd been and what I'd done on the previous afternoon. "I looked in at the motel room door just before the ambulance came to take her away and saw that she was holding the gun in her left hand. My cousin wasn't left-handed. She always used to tease me mercilessly because I was a leftie when we were kids."

"You and Miss Montgomery grew up together?"

"Yes, we—Freida, Georgia, and I—spent practically every summer together at Little Tombstone growing up."

"Who is Georgia?"

I was pretty sure he already knew exactly who Georgia was, but I figured it was in my best interest to play along.

"Georgia is my other cousin," I told Officer Reyes, "Second cousin, actually. She and Freida are—were—twins."

"Identical?"

"No."

"Did you and Freida get along?"

I knew where Officer Reyes was going with this, but I believe that honesty is the best policy, so I forged ahead with the truth.

"Freida and Georgia were upset that their grandmother left Little Tombstone to me instead of to them."

I decided to leave the fat investment accounts out of it. Freida had only suspected Aunt Geraldine had a stash of cash. Officer Reyes didn't need to know every detail of my Great Aunt Geraldine's financial status.

"Have either of your cousins threatened you directly?" Officer Reyes asked.

The simple answer was "yes," but without producing my grandmother's supposed confession, I couldn't tell the officer that Freida had threatened me.

"Do you suspect one or both of your cousins might have been behind the threat notes that you've received?"

"Yes, but only Freida. I'm sure Georgia had nothing to do with it."

I wondered how Georgia was taking her sister's death. Poor Georgia. Poor Abigail.

"There's something else you should know," I said. Officer Reyes had his head down in his paperwork, but he sat up straight and looked me in the eye. "That gun," I continued, "that antique gun Freida had in her hand: I think that was stolen from my aunt's apartment a couple of days ago."

"Is your late aunt's apartment currently occupied?"

"I'm occupying it. I discovered that gun a couple of days ago, among my aunt Geraldine's things, but I put it back where I'd found it. Last night I discovered that it had gone missing."

Officer Reyes scribbled furiously on the form which lay in front of him, then he asked me if I'd be willing to voluntarily submit to fingerprinting.

I said yes.

After that, since I was already in Santa Fe, I decided to go visit Juanita's mother. I'd have to make a condolence call on Abigail and Georgia sooner or later, but I wasn't ready, and I was pretty sure they weren't ready, either.

Juanita's mother lived in a memory care facility on the southern outskirts of Santa Fe. I buzzed myself into the secured unit using the code Juanita had given me and asked one of the nursing assistants to direct me to Florenza Hernandez's room.

Grandma Flo was sleeping slumped over in a chair underneath the single window in her shared room. I gently shook her awake and hoped for the best. Juanita had informed me that Grandma Flo's memory was unreliable at best, but that she remembered the old days much better than anything that had happened in recent years.

Since the old days were what I was curious about, I was hopeful that Grandma Flo might at least be able to confirm a few of my suspicions.

Grandma Flo looked up at me bleary-eyed, and it was not until after I'd plied her with several mint-chocolate wafers from the package in my tote bag that she perked up and took an interest in me.

"I'm Emma, Betty's granddaughter."

I got no flicker of recognition.

"I'm Geraldine's niece, Emma."

Grandma Flo still didn't seem to recognize me, so I pulled out one of the old photo albums from my Aunt Geraldine's and pointed to a picture of Freida, Georgia, and I standing out in front of Little Tombstone when we were all fifteen or so.

"Oh, yes, nice girls," said Grandma Flo.

I wasn't sure how well Grandma Flo could see or how well she remembered any of us. No one with all their faculties intact would ever describe Freida as a "nice girl," but maybe Juanita's mother was just too embarrassed to admit she didn't remember any of us.

"That's me," I said as I pointed to the picture, "and that's Freida, and that's Georgia. Freida and Georgia are Abigail's girls. You remember Abigail? Geraldine's daughter Abigail?"

Grandma Flo looked up at me. She appeared alert for the first time.

"Abigail's a bad girl," Grandma Flo said.

"Why is she bad?"

"She killed them," Grandma Flo said.

"Killed who?" I asked.

"Those poor people," Grandma Flo said. "That bad girl Abigail killed them."

Chapter Twenty-Two

"Who did Abigail kill? How did she kill them?" I asked Grandma Flo.

I had a hundred questions, but I wasn't going to get answers to any of them. Grandma Flo had fallen asleep again.

I left the rest of the package of mint-chocolate wafers with the nurse at the front desk for Grandma Flo to finish later and went back out to my rental car.

When I went to put the key in the ignition, my hands were shaking. Grandma Flo's memory might come and go, but she was clearly convinced that my cousin Abigail had killed somebody, several somebodies if Grandma Flo's memory was to be relied upon.

As soon as I got back to Little Tombstone, I pulled out the manila envelope of clippings that I'd hidden underneath the mattress and found the article about the discovery of the missing Halversons' burned-out car. Then I fired up my laptop and scanned through satellite images of the landscape around Little Tombstone until I thought I'd located the spot where the Halversons' wrecked car had been discovered.

The location where the Halversons' car had been dumped was well off the beaten path, and with any luck, the scene would be more or less as it had been laying for the past fifty years or so. I intended to have a look at it myself.

I drew myself a crude map and put it in my pocket along with the article about the discovery of the Halversons' wrecked Plymouth Fury back in the early 80s. I then returned the envelope of clippings back to their hiding place. I leashed Earp and went out to the trailer court in search of Ledbetter.

While I was knocking on Ledbetter's door, Morticia stuck her head out of her Winnebago and told me that Ledbetter had gone off somewhere on his motorcycle.

"Are you busy right now?" I asked Morticia as Earp ignored us both in favor of some fascinating scent in the soil underneath Morticia's motor home.

"It's been a slow day," Morticia said. "You'd think a death in the community might make people want to find out their own fate, but for some reason, everyone's been staying away."

"I was going to ask Ledbetter to go somewhere with me," I told Morticia, "but since he's unavailable, would you be up to going on a search for clues with me?"

"Clues?"

"You'd better have a look at this," I told her and pulled the clipping out of my bag.

I tied Earp to the steps of the motor home, and Morticia led the way into the patchouli-scented interior of her Winnebago. I could understand why Earp hadn't been a fan.

"Where did you find this?" Morticia asked after she'd read the article.

"I found a whole envelope of clippings concerning this missing couple," I told her. "They were in a box of Aunt Geraldine's things."

"You think these Halverson people are the ones who were buried under the trailer court?" Morticia squinted at the article in the dim light emanating from the colored paper lantern, which hung over the dinette table that doubled as her fortune-telling booth.

"I do."

"Why don't you take this to the police, then?"

"I will," I said, "but first, I'd like more to go on than a hunch. Also, there are implications that may affect the living."

"You think someone around here killed them?"

"Possibly, but probably not intentionally."

For the first time, Morticia looked hesitant to involve herself in my search party.

"I think it was a hit and run," I said. "I don't think they were killed on purpose, but I believe whoever did it had a compelling reason to conceal the fact that this couple was dead."

"Oh?" Morticia didn't look reassured, but at least she hadn't outright refused to go with me in search of the car. "You think the car might still be there?"

"I have no idea, but given how people do things around here, and the remote area where it was dumped, I think it's very likely it was left for the past 50 years to rust away in peace. I have a map with possible locations marked. It's just a matter of checking them off one by one."

Morticia looked skeptical.

"If we don't find anything, we don't find anything," I urged her, "but I think it's worth a look."

As we bumped along the rutted road, which led to the likely location of the crushed carcass of the Halversons' Plymouth, I tried to make conversation with Morticia. I'd never spent much time alone with her, and I soon discovered that Morticia wasn't much of a talker.

"You must have a pretty good instinct about people," I said after conversation had lagged for a good five minutes.

"Most of the time."

"You must have spent at least a little time with my cousins."

"Freida and Georgia?"

"And Abigail."

"What about them?" Morticia asked.

"Mr. Wendell believes that the three of them were trying to get Aunt Geraldine declared incompetent," I told her, "They may have been trying to gain control of Aunt Geraldine's financial affairs."

"They wanted Little Tombstone?"

Morticia's tone suggested that if someone paid her to take Little Tombstone, she'd refuse the gift. I can't say I wasn't coming around to her point of view.

"It seems they did want Little Tombstone, badly enough to try and take it against my aunt's will," I said. "Aunt Geraldine never said anything about it to you?"

Morticia thought for a minute before she replied.

"Looking back on it now, I do remember her warning me not to trust your cousins. Geraldine said they were 'out to get her,' but then Geraldine was constantly getting into conflicts with Abigail, so I didn't think much about it. Geraldine never seemed all that fond of her granddaughters—well, Freida, anyway—so when she said they were 'out to get her,' I didn't take it seriously."

"We're here," I said, pulling off the side of the dirt road. "At least I think this is the right spot."

I got out of the car with my crude map and headed off down the sloping landscape in the direction I thought the car might be. After poking around in the sagebrush for fifteen minutes, it was obvious that I'd selected the wrong spot. I made the mistake of letting Earp off his leash, and I had a terrible time getting him to come back to me.

We tried four more locations before we finally found the carcass of a green Plymouth Fury. I compared it to the reference picture I'd saved to my phone. It appeared to be a 1967 model. I was comfortable in declaring that we'd found the wreck of the Halversons' car.

The car had been pushed (or driven, it was impossible to tell which) off into a small arroyo. The tires had rotted, and the front windshield was broken out. There was a large dent on the passenger side and on the roof. I was guessing that, at some point, the car had rolled.

As I circled the burned-out, rusted remains of the car, I scanned the ground. I wasn't sure what I was looking for, but since we'd driven all the way out to the middle of nowhere, I didn't want to miss a clue.

"I wonder if it was in a wreck or if it was smashed up afterward," Morticia said.

"I think it was in a wreck."

I stooped to examine the smashed-in passenger-side door, which was lightly scorched. A fire appeared to have been set on the backseat, but whoever set it seemed to have allowed it to peter out without it engulfing the vehicle.

"Look at this," I told Morticia, pointing to the dented-in passenger-side door. "The car that hit it was bright blue."

Morticia came over to look at the dented door.

"I think you're right."

We spent another twenty minutes going over the car but found nothing else of interest. I tied Earp to the bumper so I could have both hands free to take pictures of the car from various angles. I was convinced that it was the missing couple's car, but I was no closer to figuring out who had dumped it there.

When I went back to the front of the car to retrieve Earp, I found him digging in the dirt next to the deflated front tire.

"What have you got there?" I asked him.

Something red glinted in the dirt. At first, I thought it might be a piece of broken taillight. I didn't want Earp to cut his paws, so I untied him and handed him off to Morticia.

I used a stick to dig out the object. It was a hood ornament. The chrome was pocked with age, and the red emblem in the center was considerably faded.

"What do you think this is?" I asked Morticia as I held up the object for her inspection. "This car still has its hood ornament."

"Looks like a hood ornament to me, too," Morticia said. "But don't ask me what kind it is."

Chapter Twenty-Three

When we returned to Little Tombstone, it was almost dark. I noticed that lights were on in the Curio Shop and the Museum of the Unexplained, so I surmised that Hank was back home from the hospital.

The previous day, a crew of men in protective suits had rid the premises of bees. I hoped that Hank would suffer no lingering effects from his brush with death.

The bell on the door jingled as I went inside the Curio Shop, but it took several minutes for Hank to emerge from his tiny apartment in the back.

In the meantime, Earp and I made a tour of the premises, which didn't seem much worse for the wear after having a crew of exterminators tromping all over it. Of course, Hank's system of organization was a complete mystery to me, so there might have been scores of things out of place. It looked like a lot of piles of faded pseudo-southwestern tchotchkes to me, but doubtless, Hank felt otherwise.

"How are you feeling, Hank?" I asked him when he finally made an appearance.

Except for a lot of pink spots remaining on his face and neck, Hank looked remarkably normal.

I've heard that a near-death experience will often inspire a person to take a fresh look at life and how they are living it. Some people take it as a wake-up call to cultivate kindness, gentleness, and generosity. This did not appear to be the case with Hank.

He was crankier than I'd ever seen him.

"I ought to sue you," were his first words.

"I'm very sorry about what happened," I told Hank. "We're trying to determine who put the bees' nest in your shop."

"How am I to know it wasn't you?" Hank pointed an accusatory finger at me.

His hand trembled, and I hoped he wasn't about to pass out on me.

"Are you sure you are feeling well enough to be up and around?" I asked him. "Wouldn't it be better if you stayed with your friend Phyllis, so she can keep an eye on you?"

"You'd like that, wouldn't you?" Hank said. "That was your little plan all along. You want me to go away long enough so you can empty out this place and put me and everything I own on the street."

I had to suppress a smile at the thought of everything Hank owned on the street. It would bring traffic through Amatista to a standstill.

"Your great aunt would turn over in her grave if she only knew how you were treating such a loyal friend," Hank continued. "After all I've done for her—"

"I have no intention of evicting you," I tried to reassure Hank. "You've been here for years. Little Tombstone wouldn't be the same without you."

"That's not what Freida told me."

Surely Hank knew Freida was dead, but I decided not to bring it up just in case he hadn't yet heard. In his present mood, he'd probably accuse me of being the one who killed her.

"What did Freida tell you?"

"She told me you planned to knock this place down and put in one of those big truck stops."

Replacing Little Tombstone with a truck stop probably wasn't a bad idea, from a business standpoint, but I was certain that wasn't what my Aunt Geraldine had in mind when she left me the place. I tried my best to reassure Hank that I had no plans for major changes to Little Tombstone. Hank appeared moderately mollified, so I decided to press my luck and pump him for information.

"You've lived here for a long time. How many years has it been?"

"I opened up the shop in 1968."

That was over a decade before the Halversons had gone missing.

"Do you remember anything about this?" I asked him as I handed him the clipping about the discovery of the Halversons' missing car.

"Yep," Hank said. "I remember that."

"What do you think happened to the Halversons?"

"Dunno. Never met the people."

According to one of the early articles concerning the Halversons' mysterious disappearance, they hadn't lived long in Amatista before they went missing, so Hank's protest that he'd never met them was believable.

"Any theories, hunches, suspicions? There must have been a lot of talk when they disappeared."

"You don't think I had anything to do with it, do you?"

Hank's voice was very high and shrill, and his already-pink face was considerably pinker. It had never entered my mind that Hank had had anything to do with the Halversons' disappearance, but I suddenly started to wonder if he might have.

"Of course, I don't think you had anything to do with the Halversons going missing," I said. "It's just that you've lived around here for a long time. I thought you might have seen something or heard rumors."

"I don't listen to rumors," Hank said as if that settled the matter.

Maybe Hank didn't listen to rumors, but he was all ears when it came to conspiracy theories, so I decided that desperate times called for desperate measures.

"You know," I said, "some people have gone so far as to suggest that the Halversons were Soviet agents. Do you think that's why they were killed?"

I was 'some people', but Hank didn't need to know that I was quite possibly the only one who'd ever suggested the Halversons were Russian spies.

"That's a bunch of baloney," Hank said. "Greg Halverson was an auto mechanic, and his Missus was a housewife. Nicest people you ever met."

"I thought you'd never met them?"

"I didn't," Hank said defensively. "That's just what people said."

"So, you don't think there's any possibility that those bodies that were buried under the trailer court might be the missing Halversons?"

"Listen," Hank said, coming closer and prompting Earp, who'd been nosing about among the labyrinth of kachina dolls propped against a display case of "Zuni" pottery of questionable provenance, to come and lean protectively against my ankles. When Hank got a couple of feet away, Earp started to growl. "There's no good comes from digging up anyone's past sins,"

148

Hank continued as he stepped even closer, "it'll just end up coming back to bite the living in the—"

"Thank you, Hank, for your valuable input," I said as I backed out the door with my hand firmly clutching Earp's collar.

Hank had already been attacked by a swarm of bees. Being bitten on the leg by an elderly pug would be adding insult to injury.

Clearly, Hank knew a lot more about the disappearance of the Halversons than he was telling me. He'd all but admitted that he believed the missing couple had been buried underneath the trailer court, but I was pretty sure Hank would never repeat that suspicion to anyone wearing a badge.

It was fully dark by the time I was done dealing with Hank, so I took Earp upstairs. I was starving, but I had one more task to perform before I went down to the Bird Cage Café to have some supper.

I went around to the back of the motel, where Uncle Ricky's old Cutlass Supreme was rusting away quietly under a ripped tarp. I pulled up the front of the tarp covering the hood and shone the light from my phone onto where the hood ornament should have been but wasn't.

The hood ornament appeared to have been broken off, rather than unscrewed from its position, so I took the hood ornament I'd found next to the Halverson's wrecked Plymouth and fitted it to the broken bit protruding from the hood of the Cutlass.

The hood ornament fit to the broken shaft perfectly. There was no longer any doubt in my mind that, somehow, Uncle Ricky's Cutlass had been involved in pushing the Halversons' car off into the arroyo.

My suspicions confirmed, I went to the Bird Cage for supper.

Morticia's business might have suffered in the wake of Freida's death, but the Bird Cage Café's business certainly hadn't. The place was packed.

"You'll have to wait or go with takeout," Chamomile told me, "unless you're willing to share a table with somebody."

I looked around the room. Most of the tables were crowded with couples or families, but I saw one solo diner in the corner.

Nancy Flynn was contemplating an untouched plate of enchiladas. She didn't notice me until I spoke to her.

"Mind if I join you?" I asked.

Her expression said she did mind, but her mouth said she didn't, so I took a seat across from her and signaled for Chamomile to come over and take my order.

After Chamomile had gone off to the kitchen with my request for chicken tamales with salsa verde, I turned my attention to Nancy.

"I found something interesting when I was going through my Aunt Geraldine's things," I said.

Nancy barely acknowledged my statement. She had shifted to the edge of her seat and was chowing down on her enchiladas as if she were a contestant in a speed-eating contest. I wanted to tell her that was no way to savor the best chicken enchiladas north of the border, but I doubted she'd take it well.

"I found a map of Little Tombstone," I told Nancy. "It looked a lot like a treasure map. I remember my Uncle Ricky being big into metal detecting. Do you think he was looking for something?"

Halfway through my little speech, Nancy had started choking. I reached over to pound her on the back before I continued.

"It's just that I came across this newspaper clipping about a cache of stolen gold coins thought to have been buried somewhere in the area."

Nancy had stopped coughing, finally. She was still very red in the face, though. She took a long swig of water before she replied.

"I have a vague recollection of hearing some of the old-timers tell stories about a stagecoach robbery."

"Do you think the story is true?"

Chapter Twenty-Four

"Who knows?" Nancy said. "If the story of the stagecoach robbery is true, somebody probably found the gold years ago."

"Wouldn't a discovery like that be hard to hide?" I asked. "The article I read put the value of the gold coins at around $200,000 in today's dollars, well 1998's dollars, anyway."

Nancy had taken another bite.

"That was what my Uncle Ricky was looking for, wasn't it? That was the windfall he was hoping for?"

Nancy waited until she finished chewing before she replied.

"Yes, he was looking for that gold, but he never found it. Not a single coin."

"Are you sure? Is it possible he might have hidden his find from you?"

"No," Nancy was emphatic. "We told each other everything."

"If Uncle Ricky had been involved in something illegal, you would have known?"

Nancy was choking again. I repeated the procedure of pounding her on the back. At this rate, half of those enchiladas were going to go down the wrong way.

"Your Uncle Ricky wasn't involved in any shady dealings," Nancy insisted. "Those debts he racked up were the result of overspending and a couple of unfortunate business deals."

"No shady dealings?" I persisted.

"Not on his part. Your Uncle Ricky was just too trusting, and he never was very good at keeping a rein on his expenses."

"You're sure Uncle Ricky wasn't involved in anything shady at all? Not even the disposal of a couple of dead bodies?"

Nancy stood to her feet. Her plate was still half-full, but I could see she had no intention of staying to finish. I could see the bulge under her denim jacket. Just as Ledbetter had suggested, Nancy was carrying a concealed weapon. I decided to change the subject.

"Ledbetter tells me you know a lot about guns," I said. "I was curious about Uncle Ricky's old revolver. You know the one I'm talking about?"

"No," Nancy said.

I didn't believe her. I could have continued shouting questions at her retreating back, but there didn't seem to be much point. As Nancy passed the register by the door, she slapped a twenty down on the counter and yelled at Chamomile, who was three tables away, that she was paying her bill, and that Chamomile could keep the change.

After I'd finished my own supper, I paid my bill and went into the kitchen in search of Juanita.

"I'm going to have to fire that boy," Juanita said without even saying hello.

"Marco?"

"He hasn't shown up for work for three days now," Juanita said. "Pastor Freddy says he doesn't know what's wrong with him. Marco claims to have the flu but refuses to let his father take him to the doctor."

I slept fitfully that night. So did Earp. At three in the morning, I was awakened by a crash in the kitchen. Earp had woken up, jumped down from his spot at the end of my bed and somehow managed to scramble onto a dining chair. He'd gotten at the bag of dog treats I had unwisely left out on the kitchen counter.

In the process, Earp had knocked a ceramic bowl and a plastic glass to the floor. The bowl had broken. That's what woke me.

After I'd cleaned up the mess and given Earp a midnight snack of the kibble I'd selected because the bag promised it was perfectly suited to Sedentary Senior Dogs, I wasn't a bit sleepy.

Earp turned his nose up at the bowl of diet kibble and went grumbling back to bed.

I decided to tackle the box of tax forms I'd found in the back of Aunt Geraldine's closet.

The tax forms—no surprise—were not a riveting read. I started with the file marked 1985.

According to the tax forms, signed by both my Aunt Geraldine and my Uncle Ricky, Little Tombstone had been operating at a loss. My Aunt Geraldine and Uncle Ricky's personal finances were in barely better shape. The same was true of 1986, 1987, 1988, 1989, and 1990. Nothing changed in 1991 except that the 1991 return was signed only by Aunt Geraldine. Uncle Ricky had died the summer of that year.

On the 1992 return, everything was different; Little Tombstone was finally making a profit. One could be forgiven for assuming that Uncle Ricky had been the factor weighing down the business, but I believed otherwise.

I retrieved the graph-paper treasure map from underneath the mattress and double-checked the date beside the large star marking what I believed was the location where my Aunt Geraldine had unearthed the hidden gold. It said January 23, 1992.

I skimmed through another ten years' worth of tax returns. Every single one showed Little Tombstone operating at a substantial—albeit not wildly unrealistic—profit. Then, around 2002, Little Tombstone had gone back to losing money. However, my Aunt's personal tax returns told quite a contrasting story; she'd been taking modest withdrawals from her investment accounts to live on.

I fired up my laptop and used the login information that Mr. Wendell had given me to access the accounts that Ledbetter had maintained for my aunt. The trajectory of growth on the accounts amounted to some million and a half dollars. The modest amount my Aunt took out each year to live on had been more than replaced by new growth each year. Clearly, Ledbetter was something of a stock-picking genius.

By the time I finally fell asleep, it was getting light. I was woken up mid-morning by the ringing of my phone. It was Officer Reyes on the other end.

"I thought you might be relieved to know," he said stiffly, "that you are no longer a suspect in your cousin's death."

No one had bothered to inform me I was a suspect in the first place, but I decided to let it go.

"The fingerprints on the antique Colt were a perfect match for you," Officer Reyes said, "but the results of the autopsy showed your cousin died of a single bullet to the head."

I wasn't at all sure how that conclusively ruled me out as a suspect, but I kept listening.

"The bullet that killed your cousin was a 9mm. She was shot with a different gun. The forensic analysis also suggests that she was shot from a distance of ten to twenty feet."

Interesting.

"What kind of guns take 9mm bullets?" I asked.

"The bullet could have come from any number of modern handguns," Officer Reyes said. "It doesn't get us any closer to finding your cousin's killer, but it is clear that the antique revolver was planted at the scene."

After Officer Reyes hung up, I was in no mental state to doze off again, so I got dressed and took Earp out back to answer the call of nature.

After Earp had done his business, I knocked on the door of Ledbetter's trailer. When he answered, I told him what Officer Reyes had told me about the bullet that had killed Freida.

"Do you know anybody around here who carries a 9mm handgun?" I asked him.

"I carry one," said Ledbetter, "I have a Beretta. I keep it next to my bed when I'm sleeping, and I stick it in my saddlebag when I take my bike out."

I didn't think Ledbetter would be so forthcoming with that information if he were the one who'd shot Freida, so I asked, "Anybody else? Does Hank carry a handgun?"

"Hank hates guns," Ledbetter said. "As a boy, his father was killed in a hunting accident, so he refuses to touch firearms."

"Oh, what about Nancy?"

"Nancy carries a 9mm Luger," Ledbetter said.

"Do you think she could have shot Freida?" I asked. "Officer Reyes said Freida was shot from a distance."

"How would that even be possible?" Ledbetter asked. "Freida was found inside a room in the motel."

"I think it's time we took another look at room one," I said.

Ledbetter walked me over to the motel, but he didn't seem awfully eager to go inside room one.

"I'll keep an eye on Earp while you snoop around," he told me. "I really don't believe you are going to find anything. The police already went over the place with a fine-tooth comb."

Inside room one, everything appeared exactly as it had last I had seen it, minus Freida's body sprawled across the old mattress in the middle of the floor. There was a tiny dark brown stain on the mattress where blood had trickled from the wound in my cousin's head. I tried not to look at it.

I surveyed the perimeter of the room, trying to figure out how anyone could have managed to shoot Freida from a distance. Of course, there was the possibility that someone had shot her elsewhere and then moved the body into the motel.

This theory was complicated by the fact that several people had heard gunshots. In fact, the sound of shots was what had summoned Oliver to room one in the first place, but it was always possible that whoever had killed Freida might have moved her body and then fired off a gun to make it seem as if she'd just been shot.

The only possible point of entry for a bullet, if Freida had died inside the motel room, was through a broken window facing the road which passed by Little Tombstone and continued to the cemetery. That road ended at the gated entrance to Nancy Flynn's ranch.

I was about to go out and look around for possible places the shooter might have been standing when I noticed a bit of splintered wood on the underside of the trim around the windowsill. I went closer to investigate.

"Come in and take a look at this," I called out to Ledbetter.

Chapter Twenty-Five

Ledbetter came inside reluctantly, dragging an equally reluctant Earp behind him. Earp strained in the direction of the mattress, and when Ledbetter let him, he went over and started sniffing so vigorously I thought he might hyperventilate.

"Did you find anything?" Ledbetter asked.

"Look at that," I said and pointed to the splintered windowsill.

I took Earp's leash so Ledbetter could squat down and examine the wood. The damage was barely visible when standing.

Ledbetter prodded the spot with his finger, then took out his pocketknife.

"Do you think that's a bullet in there?" I asked.

He nodded.

"Maybe we should leave it be until the police can take a look," I said.

"You're probably right about that."

Ledbetter put his knife away. As he moved back from the window, he stepped on a floorboard that squeaked, which attracted the attention of the already overwrought Earp. The pug darted over and started nosing around the floorboards. I went over and put a dog treat in front of his nose. While Earp was wolfing it down, I examined the board. It looked loose. I found an old table knife lying nearby and used it to pry up the corner of the board.

When I removed the board, I found nothing but dirt underneath.

"Do you think this was a hiding place?" I asked Ledbetter.

"Maybe," he said. "Or it might just be a loose board. This place is practically falling down around our heads."

He was right about that.

The ground underneath the board was far looser than I would have expected desert soil to be after sitting under a building for over fifty years.

"Want to try this?" Ledbetter handed me an old spoon he'd found in the piles of junk scattered around the room.

I took the spoon and dug around in the loose soil, but I found nothing except some rusty nails and an old button. Regardless, I was convinced that, up until quite recently, something had been hidden there underneath the floorboards.

"I'd better call Officer Reyes," I told Ledbetter, "and have him send someone out to have a look at this second bullet. Maybe they already found it, but he didn't mention it to me, so it's better to be sure."

After I'd parted ways with Ledbetter and called Officer Reyes, I turned my attention to the thing I'd been dreading most: visiting Abigail and Georgia.

I texted Abigail and got no reply. Georgia, however, replied back right away and suggested that we meet in a little coffee shop in Santa Fe.

Three hours later, I was sitting on the second-story terrace of an old adobe building in the historic district. It was a beautiful sunny fall day, and I was basking in the sunshine, eyes closed against the bright light, when I felt a tap on my shoulder.

It was Georgia. I wanted to hug my cousin, but we're not a family of huggers, so I shuffled around awkwardly and ended up slapping her on the back.

"I'm so sorry about your sister," I said.

Georgia mumbled something under her breath—I think it was "thanks"—and asked me if I'd ordered.

After that, we digressed into small talk. I asked Georgia how her little boy was doing—she had a six-year-old named Maxwell—and she asked me how I was settling down at Little Tombstone. This went on for ten minutes while we waited for our coffees.

After the coffees arrived, I got to the point.

"I'd like to talk about Freida's death," I said, "if you're up to it."

Georgia nodded stiffly.

"I was a suspect for a short time," I said.

This appeared to be news to Georgia.

"Why would they think you did it?" she asked.

"Freida was holding your grandfather's antique revolver in her hand when her body was discovered. Someone stole that revolver from the apartment not long before Freida died, and my fingerprints were on it, so the police figured—"

"But why would anyone think you'd want to kill Freida? Do they think just because we were contesting the will—"

I noticed that Georgia was using the past tense. Had Freida been the sole driving force behind the campaign to gain control of Little Tombstone?

"The police don't know about this," I said as I withdrew my grandmother's supposed confession letter from my handbag, "but if they had, this alone would have been enough to convince them I had a motive." I handed the letter over to Georgia before I continued. "A few days before Freida died, she came by Little Tombstone and informed me that I must relinquish all claims on Little Tombstone, or she was taking that letter to the police and the press."

Georgia read through the letter and then, to my shock, took it and tore it up in little bits, right there at the table.

"It's clearly fake," she said, "Freida must have typed up that letter and forged Aunt Betty's signature."

Georgia stuffed the pieces of torn paper one by one into the remains of her coffee, replaced the plastic lid and shook it a little.

"There," she said. "That's taken care of."

I supposed that it was, but what I didn't understand was how completely confident Georgia could be that my grandmother had nothing to do with the untimely disappearance of the Halversons.

"I know who did it," Georgia said. "I know who killed the Halversons. It wasn't your grandmother."

"Who was it?"

"It was a hit-and-run, but from what I understand, it wouldn't have changed anything if the person who hit them hadn't panicked. Both the Halversons died at the scene shortly after the collision."

"How do you know all this?"

Georgia pressed her lips together and lapsed into silence.

"I'm pretty sure those bones they dug up from under the trailer court are the remains of the Halversons," I told Georgia. "I assume you've heard about that."

"I did," Georgia said. "Freida said there was a broken water main or something. She was shocked there were bodies buried at Little Tombstone."

"Freida didn't know how the Halversons died?"

"Freida didn't know a lot of things. Freida wasn't the sort to be trusted with sensitive information, so nobody told her."

I decided I wasn't going to get any more clarity about the demise of the Halversons out of Georgia, so I moved on to the horrible main topic.

162

"I was there at the scene," I said, "shortly after Freida died, and I'm having a very hard time believing it was a suicide."

"That's what the detective told us, too," Georgia was looking a bit pale. She'd been idly drawing lines with her finger in some sugar that had spilled on the tabletop. I noticed her hands were shaking.

I was glad she hadn't been at Little Tombstone to see what I had seen.

"Officer Reyes told me that the autopsy concluded that she died from a single gunshot wound," I told Georgia, "but that the bullet that killed her couldn't have possibly come from Uncle Ricky's antique revolver. It came from a weapon of modern make."

"I know."

I waited for Georgia to say something else, but she didn't. Instead, she stopped drawing lines in the spilled sugar and put her hands in her lap.

"Is there anyone who might have wanted Freida dead?" I asked. It was a terrible question to ask, but there seemed no point in tiptoeing around the issue.

"Lots of people were probably pretty happy to hear that she'd died," Georgia said. "I know that's a horrible thing to say, but it's the truth. My sister had a special talent for making people hate her."

"But you can't think of anyone who hated her enough to kill her?"

"Look," said Georgia, her voice rising. "Sometimes it's better to leave well enough alone."

I'd never seen my cousin Georgia cry, not even when we were kids, but she was crying now.

"I know that you know who killed Freida," I said. I hadn't meant to say those words out loud; they just came tumbling out. "Why won't you tell?"

Chapter Twenty-Six

When I accused Georgia of knowing who'd killed her twin, my cousin sprang to her feet so fast she knocked her metal chair over with a clatter. Other patrons were staring, and a barista came out to make sure everyone was all right.

When Georgia had righted her chair, the barista had gone away, and everyone else had stopped staring, my cousin and I sat down once more.

"Emma, you've got to let this one go," Georgia pleaded.

"Why?"

"Freida wasn't murdered."

"She was shot point-blank, execution-style," I protested. "How can that be categorized as anything but murder?"

"I can't tell you anything more," Georgia said. "But you have to trust me. The person who killed Freida only did it to prevent someone else from dying."

"Who?"

"I can't tell you that, either."

"Why?"

"You already know too much."

Georgia stared down at the tabletop as if its shiny surface contained the secrets of the universe.

"How do you know what happened to Freida?" I demanded. "It's almost as if you were there or something."

"I was there," said Georgia.

"I showed up within minutes of the shooting. I didn't see you."

"I was supposed to be meeting Freida, but I got there early, and she wasn't expecting me. After the shooting, I didn't want anyone to see me, so I made myself scarce. I didn't want to have to answer any questions."

"Are you willing to walk down to the Saint Francis Cathedral and swear in front of the altar that you had nothing to do with Freida getting shot?"

"Yes. Absolutely."

"You don't have to do that," I said. "I believe you."

I did believe Georgia. I just didn't believe she was right about letting whoever shot her twin in the head walk away a free man.

When I got back to Little Tombstone, the police were there, going over room one again. They went away shortly after. Officer Reyes didn't say anything to me before they went. I hoped that didn't mean that I'd somehow regained my status as a suspect.

I couldn't stop thinking about what Georgia had told me. Her insistence that Freida hadn't been murdered made no sense.

I decided to try and confirm Georgia's claim that she'd been at Little Tombstone when Freida was shot, but when I made the circuit of the residents, no one remembered seeing her.

I did gain a few other bits of interesting information, however.

Juanita reminded me that Marco had been throwing up near the dumpster shortly after the shooting. I made a mental note to go over that area with a fine-tooth comb.

Oliver also reported seeing Nancy Flynn's pickup tearing past on the road to her ranch as he rounded the corner of the motel a minute or two after he'd heard gunfire, but there was nothing terribly unusual about that. Nancy Flynn always raised a cloud of dust when she went past, which was generally several times a day.

I also asked around to see if it seemed that Abigail, Freida, or Georgia might have been searching Little Tombstone for Aunt

Geraldine's hidden stashes of gold—not that I believed that much, if any, remained concealed around the place.

Still, I might know that my aunt had long since liquidated her treasure to cash, but I didn't think my cousins had known there was no longer anything of value hidden on the premises.

When I quizzed them, Hank, Juanita, and Ledbetter could all recall instances of suspicious behavior on both Abigail and Freida's part, but no one seemed to think Georgia had been intent on ransacking the place.

"What is it that you suspect they were looking for?" Juanita had asked me.

It was a fair question, but not one I was willing to answer.

While pumping Hank for information, I realized right away that he knew exactly what I was getting at.

"I don't think they knew about the gold," Hank said, "but I wouldn't put it past those women to have been sticking their noses in where they didn't belong. There's none of it left, you know. Not unless Geraldine decided to keep a piece or two as a souvenir. I have one. It was a gift from your aunt, so don't think I'm going to give it to you."

I told Hank I wouldn't dream of laying claim to his gold piece, but that I'd like to see it. He grunted and shuffled back to his tiny living quarters. I heard a lot of scraping and thuds as if Hank were moving furniture around. Apparently, Hank kept his valuables well hidden.

"How did my aunt manage to unload that much gold without anybody finding out?" I asked when Hank returned.

He held out the coin to me, and I took it from him. I noticed Hank was keeping an eagle eye on me as if convinced I was planning to pocket the gold piece the moment he relaxed his vigilance.

"I helped Geraldine out a little," Hank said. "That's why I get my rent at a discount."

It was more like he got his rent free, but I didn't think pointing that out would go over well.

"I can't tell you the details," Hank added.

"Oh? Why not?"

My aunt must have technically cheated the taxman; it was clear she'd never declared her treasure trove. However, it also appeared that she'd run practically every penny's worth through Little Tombstone's books, which meant that Uncle Sam had eventually ended up with his cut, one way or another.

It surprised me that my aunt had bothered to make an illegal act ethical. Then again, perhaps, she'd had some other motivation for laundering her treasure trove that I was yet to discover.

"I can't tell you how I helped her," Hank said, "because it involves a third party."

"Oh," I said and left it at that. "When am I going to get to meet this lady friend of yours?" I was terribly curious to find out what kind of woman would link her lot to the likes of Hank Edwards. "Does she live around here?"

"Phyllis lives in Santa Fe," Hank said stiffly.

"Is she retired?"

"Sort of."

"Oh, what does she do?"

"She owns a small business."

"Is she also in the souvenir trade?"

That was the nicest way of putting it I could think of, but it didn't seem to mollify Hank.

"You know, you're an awfully nosy woman," Hank said.

I wondered what my gender had to do with it, but I decided not to pursue the subject further. Hank was clearly uncomfortable with talking about his lady friend's line of work.

"What's Phyllis's last name?" I asked.

I left without an answer because Hank picked up a probably-made-in-China kachina doll, which he looked ready to hurl at my head.

The next morning, I returned to the Museum of the Unexplained to try again. I had lots of other unanswered questions: ones far more pressing than the nature of Phyllis's business ventures.

This time, I came bearing gifts: powdered sugar-dusted donuts I'd bought from the truck stop five miles north.

"I prefer the kind with jelly inside," Hank informed me, but he ate three anyway.

After that, I let Hank have his head on the topic of chupacabras. It wasn't until I'd been thoroughly educated on the feeding and breeding habits of the mythical species that I introduced a more sensitive subject.

"You're the only one around Little Tombstone who knows about the gold, right?" I asked.

"Far as I know, but like I said, my lips is sealed."

"There's something else you might be the only one who knows about," I said.

"Oh?" Hank looked wary. I handed him another donut and shot another pointedly admiring glance in the direction of his stuffed chupacabra collection.

"It's about those bodies buried under the trailer court," I said, trying not to shudder as I tore my attention away from the taxidermied leer of Papa Chupacabra and the oddly haughty glass-eyed stare of Mama Chupacabra.

"I'm sure it's going to turn out those bones belong to the Halversons," I told Hank. "What do you know about how they disappeared?"

"I don't know nothin'," Hank insisted.

"Morticia and I took an interesting little excursion the other day," I said. "We went out to where the Halversons' car was dumped. It's remarkably well preserved, considering it's been sitting there in the elements for over fifty years."

Chapter Twenty-Seven

Hank maintained a stony silence when I told him Morticia and I had been out to take a looked at the Halversons' wrecked car.

"I took some pictures of the car," I told Hank. "Would you like to see them?"

Hank didn't say no, so I pulled up the photos of the wrecked car on my phone, shoved it under his nose and started scrolling through them.

When I got to the picture of the hood ornament I'd found next to the car, I paused.

"I found it very odd," I said, "that there'd be a hood ornament for a Cutlass Supreme sitting next to the wreck of the Halversons' Plymouth Fury."

Hank grunted, but he didn't offer any other verbal input.

"The only thing I can figure," I said, "was that the Cutlass was used to nudge the Halversons' vehicle down over the edge of the arroyo, and, in the process, the hood ornament of the Cutlass got broken off. What do you think?"

"Look," said Hank, pushing my phone away with his hand. "You are a very stupid woman to go around asking questions after all these years. What good do you think it's going to do for anyone to find out what really happened to the Halversons?"

"Don't you think their family deserves to know?"

"The Halversons don't have no family."

"Are you sure? No children? No parents? No siblings?"

"They didn't have no kids. If their parents are still living, which I doubt, they'd be over a hundred by now. Greg was an only child, and I heard Stacy has a sister, but Phyllis says the sister's got Alzheimer's and don't even know her own name."

I kept my mouth shut and hoped Hank would keep talking.

He did.

"Look," said Hank. "If you're just trying to satisfy your curiosity, I'll tell you this much: I did see that Plymouth of the Halversons' getting towed off by your Uncle Ricky with that old Blue Cutlass that's still parked out back of the motel. The whole thing probably did happen more or less like you said, but I wish you'd get it through your head that it's better to leave sleeping dogs lie. Otherwise, you're likely to be the one that gets bit."

Letting sleeping dogs lie seemed to be a real favorite with Hank. I let the subject go.

"Seen any more lights at night?" I asked Hank.

Hank's face lit up.

"No!" he said. "You and that Australian kid must've really scared some sense into those extraterrestrials."

Oliver and I had scared sense into somebody, but I was pretty sure those somebodies weren't alien life forms.

That afternoon, my cousin Abigail finally texted me back. She was free that afternoon, and, if I wanted, I was welcome to stop by her house.

My cousin never married. I suspect she couldn't find a man prepared to take on Georgia and, especially, Freida.

Abigail lived in a historic high-rent district in Santa Fe. Abigail was in real estate, and she'd done very well for herself. I couldn't figure out why she'd been so eager to get her paws on Aunt Geraldine's money. Abigail had plenty of her own, or at least that's how it looked. Perhaps, Abigail was one of those people who are never satisfied, no matter how much they amass.

Parking was a problem. The streets were super narrow in Abigail's neighborhood, and she'd specifically warned me not to block the alley, so I left my rental car six blocks away at a convenience store and walked. It was sunny but chilly, and I pulled the collar of my jacket up and wished I had worn a scarf.

I rang the bell on the outside of the adobe-walled courtyard. It took a while for Abigail to come out of the house and let me in.

Georgia, Georgia's son, Maxwell, and Freida had all been living with Abigail for the past several years. I wondered how Abigail was coping with her daughter's death.

Not well, judging by her swollen eyes when she finally came out, opened the wooden gate, and ushered me across the tiled patio.

"I'm very sorry about what happened to Freida," I said, after Abigail had bustled around and brought me a mineral water, opened the curtains a little wider, and removed some invisible dust from the row of business awards she kept on the mantle of the fireplace in the living room.

Abigail finally sat down, but she remained fidgety.

"I don't know why people keep saying how sorry they are," Abigail said. "Why are you apologizing for something that isn't your fault?"

Abigail said it like she wasn't totally convinced that Freida's death wasn't at least a little bit my fault. I wondered if the police had let on that I was briefly considered a suspect, or maybe Georgia had told Abigail that I'd fallen under suspicion.

"I think people are just trying to express their sadness," I said.

"But they aren't sad," Abigail persisted. "Hardly anybody is sad that Freida is gone. Probably, Georgia misses her, and I certainly do, but the truth is that Freida wasn't the sort of person who inspired fondness."

Abigail was right about that, but it seemed cruel to agree with her, so I took a long, awkward swig of mineral water and waited for my cousin to keep talking.

"It's my fault," she said. "You pass on your bad traits to your children, even if you don't want to."

At this point, Abigail noticed more invisible dust, this time on the bookcase. She got up and ran her fingers over the exposed shelf.

"I've done things I deeply regret," she told me, "and now I guess I'm paying for it."

I wanted to ask what those lamented actions were, but I couldn't bring myself to ask a grieving mother a question like that.

"You probably have no idea," Abigail said without prompting. "No one in the family ever speaks of it, but when I was very young, I killed someone. Two people actually."

I've been told I have a sympathetic face, but normally people don't break down and admit to killing anyone. Half of me wanted my cousin Abigail to bare her soul, and half of me was regretting having come in the first place. I'd had my suspicions, but now that it appeared they were about to be confirmed, I wasn't so sure I shouldn't have taken Hank Edwards' advice to keep my "nose out of other people's business."

"I didn't mean for anyone to get hurt," Abigail continued. "I'd had a few drinks, but I thought I was fine to drive. I was only sixteen. So clueless—"

Abigail had to be talking about the Halversons.

"I shouldn't have left them there like that," she said. "I'm almost certain they were already dead, but still, I shouldn't have—"

Abigail was crying now. I hoped she wasn't going to get hysterical.

"We've all done things we regret," I said. "We were all once young and stu—naive."

"You don't understand," Abigail said. "I was horrible to my mother."

I wondered if she was talking about back when she was sixteen or more recent events.

Then, quite abruptly, I was dismissed. Abigail thanked me for coming, subjected me to the world's most awkward one-armed hug, and walked me back out to the gate.

When I got back to the convenience store, I went inside and bought the biggest bag of chocolate candy they had, then headed over to the care center where Juanita's mother was living.

I buzzed myself in at the locked entrance and went to Grandma Flo's room. Grandma Flo was dozing when I came in, but she woke up enough for me to feed her a couple of chocolates. By chocolate number three, she still didn't remember who I was, and without the aid of pictures, it was difficult to jog her memory of who Abigail was, either.

I finally resorted to leading questions, something I was trying to avoid.

"Did you ever know anyone who killed another person?" I asked Grandma Flo.

She stopped gumming her chocolate and looked up at me with her faded watery eyes.

"It's bad to kill somebody," she said.

Chapter Twenty-Eight

"Did you know any bad people like that when you were younger?" I asked Grandma Flo.

"That bad girl—" she answered. "I knew a bad girl—"

Flo appeared to be falling asleep again.

"Did it have to do with a car?" I asked.

"She hit them," Grandma Flo roused herself enough to say, "She crashed right into them and left them lying there."

"Where, where did she leave them?"

Grandma Flo wasn't listening; I might as well have been talking to myself.

"Then she run away to have babies. Didn't have any husband, though—"

I was convinced that Grandma Flo was talking about Abigail, but nothing I asked could induce her to come up with a name.

I fed Flo a couple more chocolates and tried again, without success, to get her to come up with a name. I finally abandoned that line of questioning.

"What did that bad girl do with those people, after she hit them with her car?" I asked.

"That Jezebel buried them."

"You mean the bad girl buried them?"

I found it very hard to believe that sixteen-year-old Abigail would have been capable of disposing of the Halversons' bodies alone. I also wondered why Grandma Flo was referring to Abigail as a Jezebel. Perhaps, it was because Abigail had been an unwed mother, but Flo had never been the type to talk so disrespectfully of other women.

"No, that Jezebel did it," Flo said.

"Not the girl who hit the people with her car?"

"No, Ricky's Jezebel. She buried them."

Now we were getting somewhere. Mrs. Gonzales's testimony would never stand up in a court of law, but I was convinced she'd just told me that Nancy Flynn had been the one who'd buried the Halversons' bodies under the trailer court at Little Tombstone.

I had already fed Grandma Flo too many chocolates, so I closed the bag and sat beside her, holding her hand until she dozed off again.

By the time I left, I was more confused than ever about what my next move should be.

When I got back to Little Tombstone, Juanita informed me that my cousin Georgia had been there looking for me.

Georgia had left me a message to meet her at Mr. Wendell's law office as soon as I got in. I wondered why she hadn't just texted me.

I went straight to Mr. Wendell's office. Georgia's son, Maxwell, was sitting on one of the chairs in the waiting room, tearing pages out of a back issue of *Farm and Ranch* and folding them into paper airplanes. I couldn't help wondering if Mr. Wendell was a *Farm and Ranch* subscriber, or if a forgetful client had abandoned the magazine in the waiting room.

"Your mother in there?" I asked Maxwell.

He nodded but didn't speak. Maxwell's not what you might call a verbal child, although Georgia claims he has a genius-level IQ.

I knocked on the door to Mr. Wendell's office, and Georgia opened the door to let me in. Mr. Wendell directed me to a chair beside Georgia.

"Your cousin has something she'd like to get off her chest," Mr. Wendell said.

Georgia didn't say anything.

"Go ahead, Miss Montgomery," Mr. Wendell prompted. "It's better if you say it in your own words."

"I'm dropping the contest to the will," said Georgia.

"Oh," I said. "That's good to know."

"Before our grandmother died, I was just going along with what Freida was pushing for. She insisted that the only reason Grams cut us out of the will was that she was going senile and didn't know what she was doing. Now I can see that was a lie. I had no idea things would get so out of hand."

"Is it true you were trying to get power of attorney before your grandmother died?" I asked.

"Yes, and I don't feel very good about that, either. When it turned out that Grams was completely in her right mind, I went behind their backs—"

"Whose backs?"

"My mother's and Freida's. I put a stop to the whole thing."

"But you still contested the will?" I couldn't help saying.

"I did," Georgia admitted. "I didn't think it was fair for you to get everything, even if Grams did have a right to be angry."

"I didn't think it was fair, either," I said, "for what it's worth."

Mr. Wendell cleared his throat loudly like he thought I'd said something I shouldn't.

"I'd like to talk to my cousin alone, if you don't mind," Georgia told Mr. Wendell.

She had a lot of nerve, kicking a lawyer out of his own office, but Mr. Wendell went without a murmur.

"I've decided to tell you everything I know about Freida's death," Georgia said after the door had closed behind Mr. Wendell.

"I'll save you the trouble," I said. "Nancy Flynn was the one who killed Freida."

Georgia stared back at me for the space of three breaths before she spoke.

"Nancy Flynn shot Freida," Georgia said. "But how did you know?"

"I didn't know for sure, but she was certainly my most likely suspect. What I don't understand is why she would do it."

"It was that kid, Marco, Juanita's dishwasher," Georgia said. "Freida was about to kill him."

"Why would Freida want to kill Marco?"

"That I don't know," Georgia admitted, "but I know what I saw with my own eyes."

"You were there in the room?"

"I was just outside the door. I arrived early, fifteen minutes before Freida had asked me to meet her. Freida didn't even know I was there. My sister had asked me to meet her in room one of the motel. She said she'd made a discovery. Freida had this nutty idea that Grams had been stashing gold pieces in various places around Little Tombstone. A few months back, Freida showed me pictures of pages out of notebook she claimed to be a record of where our grandmother had been hiding a fortune in old gold coins. According to Freida, Grams had gone so far as to hide gold inside that old cuckoo clock of hers."

Georgia clearly didn't believe the story about the hidden gold, and I didn't think it was the time nor place to enlighten her on that point.

"What happened when you reached the motel?" I asked.

"As I was coming up to the door of room one, I heard someone sobbing and pleading for his life. That door has the knob busted off, so I pushed on the door, and it swung open just enough that I could peek through the crack."

Georgia paused. I think she was summoning her courage to go on.

"When I looked inside," Georgia finally continued, "I saw Juanita's dish boy, Marco, kneeling on the floor in front of Freida. She had that old revolver of Uncle Ricky's to his head. He was begging her not to shoot, saying he wouldn't tell if she'd let him go. I don't know what that was all about, but apparently, Marco had some pretty serious dirt on my sister."

"I think I know what it was," I told Georgia, "but carry on with your story. I'll explain later."

"As I was standing there, trying to decide if I should dial 911 or burst in—I was scared that if I startled Freida, she'd end up shooting the poor kid in the head whether she'd ever intended really to kill him or not. While I was hesitating, Nancy Flynn pulled up next to the motel."

"Nancy likes to park there," I said. "I've never known her to use any other spot."

"I darted around the corner and motioned to Nancy to be quiet, then I returned to the door of room one. I expected that Nancy would follow me, but instead, she circled around to that broken window on the side of the motel and looked inside. Just as I reached the door again, intending to do something to stop Freida from hurting that boy—I wasn't sure what—Marco took matters into his own hands; he grabbed Freida by the ankles, throwing her off balance. About the same time Marco wrestled the gun away from Freida, one shot went off, and maybe a second or two later, there was another one. Freida slumped onto the mattress. I think she died instantly; at least I hope so."

Georgia had started to cry. I looked around Mr. Wendell's office for tissue, but there wasn't any.

"I'm sure she didn't suffer," I said.

Georgia got herself back under control and went on, "I honestly don't know which shot killed her."

"You're sure Nancy was outside the window when the shots went off?"

"Positive."

"It had to have been her," I said. "There was one other bullet in the motel room. I found it lodged in the woodwork around the window on the wall opposite. I haven't heard back from the police on the forensics, but I bet they will determine that it came from Uncle Ricky's revolver."

I don't know why that revelation was a relief, but it was. Nevertheless, the Santa Fe County Sheriff's department was destined to have some bewildered detectives.

"But how did Freida end up with Uncle Ricky's antique revolver in her hand?" I asked Georgia. "Was Marco the one who put it there?"

Chapter Twenty-Nine

"It was Nancy," said Georgia. "I asked her to put Gramps' revolver in Freida's hand. I wanted Freida's death to look like a suicide."

Georgia was crying in earnest now and making no effort to hide it. She had to stop for several minutes to regain her composure.

"But Nancy put it in the wrong hand," I pointed out. "Why didn't you correct her?"

"There wasn't time," Georgia said. "We heard someone coming—"

"Oliver, probably."

"We both ran. I figured no one would notice that the gun was in the wrong hand."

"I noticed. Why did you ask Nancy to make it look like a suicide?" I asked Georgia. "I mean, it's easy to see the upside for Nancy, but why would you—"

"How could our mother live with knowing she'd raised a daughter who died because she got shot by someone who was just trying to keep her from killing some poor kid?"

I could understand Georgia's line of reasoning. I'd just seen the state Abigail was in, and that was without even knowing what horrible acts her late daughter was in the act of committing when she died.

"But the detectives only found one set of fingerprints on Uncle Ricky's revolver," I said. "At least that's what they told me."

"Whose fingerprints?"

"Mine."

"Marco never touched the gun," my cousin explained. "The revolver went off when Freida dropped it as she fell. It was a chilly day. Nancy was wearing gloves. So was Freida. No prints."

I had a flashback to my Aunt Geraldine's apartment, the day Freida asked me to take out Uncle Ricky's revolver and then declined to touch it herself. I'd thought it was slightly odd at the time. Looking back on her actions now, it was clear she must have been planning for days, at least, to kill Marco with her late grandfather's revolver and make it look like I had done it. The only reason she'd asked to see that gun was so she could be sure my prints were on it.

Georgia and I lapsed into silence after that. I think we were both trying hard not to relive the scene over in our heads and failing miserably.

"I have a favor to ask," Georgia finally said.

"Wait," I said, "before we change the subject, what did Marco do after Nancy shot Freida?"

"He immediately ran out of the motel room, nearly knocked me over."

He must have gone straight to the back of the Bird Cage and started throwing up. I couldn't blame him.

"Marco must know you saw everything?" I said.

"Yes. He saw me, but I can't say for certain that he saw Nancy."

"It's entirely possible that Marco thinks the shot that killed Freida came from Uncle Ricky's revolver?"

"I suppose so."

"How would you feel about going up the hill to the Flynn ranch and having a chat with Nancy?" I asked Georgia. "I'm not sure what I want to do with what you've told me, but I think Nancy has a right to explain herself."

"You can't do that," Georgia said, her voice rising. "You can't tell anyone else anything I've said today. I told you everything in confidence."

"I know that," I said, "but it's not like we'd be disclosing any new information to Nancy."

Not much new information anyway.

"I guess it can't really make the situation worse," Georgia relented.

I suspected that same line of reasoning had factored into Georgia's decision to tell me what had really happened in room one of the motel.

"What was the favor you wanted to ask me?" I asked Georgia.

My cousin stared blankly back at me.

"You said you wanted to ask me a favor?" I repeated.

Georgia hemmed and hawed and made several false starts before I dragged it out of her. The favor she wanted was permission to move into Little Tombstone with Maxwell. She was afraid, if she continued living with her mother, she'd eventually spill the truth and break her mother's heart.

Put like that, I could hardly say no.

"You and Maxwell will have to share Aunt Geraldine's second bedroom," I told her. "I'd be happy to give up the bigger bedroom for you, but I don't think Earp would take kindly to being moved out of his habitual haunt."

Georgia and I walked out of Mr. Wendell's office to find Maxwell and Mr. Wendell having a paper airplane-flying contest. I found myself warming to the man. Maybe that Farm and Ranch subscription really was his, bought for the benefit of his agriculturally minded clients.

After we left Mr. Wendell's office, I insisted that we go straight up to see Nancy Flynn. I didn't want to give Georgia a chance to lose her nerve. I suggested we leave Maxwell with Juanita at the Bird Cage. It was several hours until the supper rush, and Maxwell could entertain himself in the dining room with the basket of toys Juanita kept behind the checkout counter for when her grandchildren stopped by for a visit.

To my surprise, Georgia went docilely along with my plan. That is, she went docilely along with my plan until we reached the locked gate to the Flynn Ranch.

We'd driven up there in my rental car, and I was personally prepared to abandon the car, climb the gate, and walk the remaining mile up to the house.

Georgia refused.

"Didn't you read the sign?" she demanded.

"What sign?"

"The one that says: 'Trespassers Will Be Shot.'"

"We're not trespassers," I pointed out. "We're neighbors."

Georgia argued that seeing as we planned to clamber over a locked gate, Nancy might not see it that way.

Georgia and I sat there waiting in the car for ten minutes before Nancy's truck came down the drive. When she reached the gate, Nancy got out of the truck and started to swing it open.

"Nancy," I said, sticking my head out the window.

"What do you want?" she snapped back. She looked irritated, but when she spotted Georgia in the passenger seat, she switched to looking scared.

"We want to talk to you," I said.

"You'd better come up to the house, then. You head on up, and I'll shut the gate behind us."

Nancy drove through the gate and backed her truck around while I started up the rocky drive to the house.

"I'm scared," said Georgia.

I figured that Nancy was just about as scared of Georgia as Georgia was of Nancy, but I was pretty sure there was no convincing my cousin of that.

When we got to the house, I parked off to the side, nose out. I think I was trying to prepare for a quick getaway, not that I was scared of Nancy or anything.

I really wasn't afraid. Nancy might have killed Freida—but given the same decision to make, assuming I'd have had Nancy's skills as a precision marksman—I might have done the same.

Nancy didn't invite us in. Instead, we all sat in a row of rockers on her front porch and rocked back and forth quietly for a few minutes before I couldn't stand the silence any longer.

"I suppose you know why we are here, Nancy," I said.

"You want me to turn myself in?"

"No!" said Georgia.

"I'm not sure what I want," I said. "Perhaps it would be best if you explain to us exactly what happened."

"It was all over in less than three minutes," Nancy said. "I pulled up, saw Georgia peeking into that motel room. She looked terrified, so I figured something bad was going on in there, so I went around to the window to assess the situation. When I saw that poor kid with a gun to his head, I knew I had to do something. I was trying to decide if I dared give Freida a warning to drop her gun when the kid went for her ankles. Just as the kid tackled her, Freida saw me in the window. I had a bead on her head. She must have pulled the trigger, just as she was knocked off her feet and dropped the gun. I'm still not certain which of us fired first. The bullet from the revolver went wild, but mine—"

Nancy broke off, unable to speak any longer.

"I know you believed you were acting for the best," Georgia said.

My cousin was sitting stiffly in her rocker, stone still and dry-eyed. I guess she'd run out of her quota of tears for the day.

"I've run over the thing in my mind a thousand times," Nancy said. "One minute I'll be wishing I hadn't pulled the trigger, but then the next minute I'll be telling myself that if the kid had died, I know I'd be wishing I had."

"I think that's a perfectly normal reaction," I said. "But why didn't you stick around and tell the police what really happened?"

"Don't know," Nancy said. "I honestly don't. I panicked, I guess. I've shot plenty of animals in my time, but never—"

She broke off again.

"It's too late to turn myself in now," Nancy finally said. "I'm begging you both to keep this incident to yourself."

Driving down the hill from the Flynn Ranch, I told Georgia I couldn't imagine what would induce Nancy to turn herself in, but that very afternoon the unthinkable happened.

Marco Fernandez had his father drive up to Santa Fe, where he walked into the Santa Fe County Sheriff's department and announced to the desk sergeant that he was prepared to confess to killing Freida Montgomery.

Chapter Thirty

As soon as I heard that Marco had confessed to killing Freida, I had Juanita call Nancy and tell her I needed to talk to her.

Fifteen minutes later, Nancy was sitting on the couch in Aunt Geraldine's apartment. Earp refrained from growling, but I noticed that he kept a sharp eye on her from his vantage point behind the TV stand.

"Now you have to tell the truth," I said after I'd explained that Marco had confessed. "You have no choice."

"Can't Marco just claim self-defense?" Nancy asked.

"That will be hard to do, seeing as the gun in Freida's hand didn't match the bullet to her head, and Marco won't be capable of coming up with a reasonable explanation for that. Marco must believe that Freida was shot during the struggle over the revolver, and he is somehow responsible."

"What I don't understand," said Nancy, "is why Freida wanted to kill that poor kid in the first place."

"I don't know for certain why Freida wanted to kill Marco," I told Nancy, "but I believe that Freida put Marco up to busting our water main, setting the kitchen on fire, and causing Hank Edwards to nearly die from being stung by bees."

"Why would he—"

"Freida was trying to drive me out of Little Tombstone," I said. "I think she paid Marco to do those things, but I suspect that after Hank ended up in the hospital, Marco got scared. I doubt, at the start, the kid intended to participate in anything more serious than minor acts of vandalism. He must have eventually realized there was no limit to how far Freida would go."

189

"That still doesn't explain why Freida would want to kill Marco," Nancy pointed out.

"I imagine Freida didn't take kindly to Marco balking at whatever she'd planned as a follow-up to the bees' nest incident. It may have been that Marco was threatening to expose the whole scheme."

I didn't say it out loud, but I couldn't help wondering if Freida hadn't initially planned to manipulate Marco into killing me, and when he refused, she decided to kill Marco instead.

I was convinced that the day Freida died, she had intended to frame me for Marco's murder, killing two birds—or in this case, two uncooperative persons—with one bullet.

"If you're not sure what to do," I suggested to Nancy, "why don't you go have a chat with Mr. Wendell and review your legal options, but please do it in a hurry. I know Marco may have caused a lot of trouble, but I don't think the poor boy deserves—"

"You're right," Nancy said. "I've done some things in my lifetime that I deeply regret, but it's too late to go back and change them now. This mistake is not too late to fix."

"My cousin Georgia will back up your story," I told Nancy. "She saw it all."

After Nancy left—she didn't tell me where she was going—I sat there absently patting Earp on the head and wondering what to do next.

I'd been doing a lot of lecturing others on the importance of "doing the right thing," but I wasn't at all sure that I'd been doing the right thing myself.

Now that I knew where Aunt Geraldine's money had come from, I didn't feel right about keeping it, but I was also uncertain who else had a right to it.

I was all but certain that my Aunt Geraldine had removed the gold from land that belonged to Nancy (although Aunt Geraldine hadn't known it), but I wasn't convinced the money from the sale of the gold ought to be returned to Nancy. Although my Uncle Ricky had been legally within his rights to dispose of the land as he chose, the way he'd gone about it had hardly been ethical. I was convinced that my grandmother had only sanctioned the transfer because she believed—wrongly, in my opinion—that it was best to shield my Aunt Geraldine from the painful truth about her husband.

Legally speaking, the original gold cache belonged to Nancy, but I couldn't bring myself to hand the money over to her. Which raised another question. The original $150,000 worth of gold coins had now grown to a fortune of over a million. Even if I wanted to return the original value of the gold, was Nancy entitled to interest?

There was also the problem of what to do about Abigail and Georgia's share of the inheritance. Would my Aunt Geraldine, were she still alive and privy to what I now knew, really still want to cut Georgia—who'd stepped in to protect her grandmother at a crucial moment—completely out of her will?

It was all too much for me. It was time to call on the collective wisdom of the Little Tombstone family.

I was just pondering how soon I could reasonably assemble all concerned parties in the dining room of the Bird Cage when Georgia arrived, complete with a howling Maxwell and six suitcases.

"There's three more in the back of the Suburban," Georgia informed me over Maxwell's protests. "I asked your handyman to bring them up."

When Oliver arrived with the suitcases, I asked him to summon Ledbetter and Hank to meet me in the dining room of the Bird Cage at 9 PM right after closing.

It was time for a moment of truth, and the truth-telling had to start with me.

Georgia was mystified by my call for a community meeting, but she agreed to come down if she could get Maxwell to sleep.

I tried calling Nancy but got no answer. I wondered if she was still consulting with Mr. Wendell. I texted her the time and place of the meeting. If she didn't show up, I'd make a decision without her.

I called Mr. Wendell's office next. He answered right away.

"I'm trying to reach Nancy Flynn," I told him.

"Miss Flynn isn't here," Mr. Wendell said so stiffly that I was certain Nancy had already come and gone. Perhaps she was currently down at the sheriff's office, confessing to her role in Freida's death.

"I'm going to need legal counsel," I told Mr. Wendell. "I have a confession to make."

"Please tell me you're not planning to confess to killing Miss Montgomery, too?"

"Certainly not," I said.

"I fail to comprehend your—"

"Be in the dining room of the Bird Cage Café tonight at nine."

"Emma—"

That was a first. Up until now, I'd been Mrs. Iverson.

"Yes, Jason."

"As your legal counselor, may I advise you not to make any hasty revelations you may later regret."

It was sound advice, but I did not take it. Instead, I belatedly asked Juanita permission to use her dining room that evening and asked her to be present.

Then I tackled my most dreaded task. I called my cousin Abigail.

Her phone was switched off.

Around 8:30, I went down to the dining room, but I was far too nervous to eat the plate of tacos Juanita insisted on setting in front of me. My ex used to joke that I could maintain my appetite in the midst of an apocalypse, but apparently, my nervous system felt what I was about to face was worse than the demise of mankind as we know it.

Shortly before nine, as the last of the diners departed, the invited participants in my little meeting began to trickle in.

By nine, everyone was present save Abigail.

"Is this about them aliens?" Hank asked when I stood up and cleared my throat for silence, although no one was talking to each other anyway.

"I have a lot of ground to cover, so I've made some notes," I said.

It was a lame way to start, but I wasn't there to compete for any public speaking awards, so I muddled on.

"I'm going to tell the truth, as I understand it, from the beginning, and if anyone wishes to correct my understanding or offer additional information, please interrupt me before I move on."

I hoped Hank wouldn't use this little meeting as an opportunity to educate us on how the Deep State, the Medical Industrial Complex, and Big Oil had been colluding to conceal that the American People had, since the fall of the Nixon

Administration, been governed by a succession of figurehead leaders controlled remotely by beings from a galaxy far, far away.

I glanced over at Hank. He was having too much difficulty getting his cigar lit to concern himself with the machinations of the Deep State.

"I'm sure you all know I recently inherited Little Tombstone from my Great Aunt Geraldine," I began.

I had everyone's complete attention, except for Hank's.

"I was surprised, as I'm sure were all of you, that Geraldine chose to leave everything she had to me, instead of leaving it to her daughter and granddaughters."

Dead silence. I knew I was currently stating the obvious, but what I was about to say would be news to (almost) everyone in the room.

"I was always supposed to receive half of Little Tombstone—the half originally belonging to my grandparents—upon Aunt Geraldine's death. What most of you don't know," I continued, "was that not only did my Great Aunt Geraldine leave me the remaining half of Little Tombstone which was originally to have gone to her daughter and granddaughters, she also left behind a small fortune."

This time, I got a bigger reaction. Nobody said anything, but everyone—except for Ledbetter—was glancing around the room as if to say, "Did **you** know?"

Ledbetter started fidgeting in his chair, like he was scared I was going to out him, but I had no intention of spilling his secrets.

"My aunt grew her wealth by a series of wise investments made with the help of a—" I tried not to look at Ledbetter, "—with the assistance of a talented financial advisor, but the source

194

of Geraldine's original nest egg is what I'd like to discuss," I continued.

I made the mistake of making eye contact with Mr. Wendell. He nodded his head in warning, but I plowed on with my revelation.

"Some of you may remember rumors of a cache of stolen gold pieces hidden near Amatista," I continued. "Fewer of you will recall that, for several years, my Uncle Ricky made a hobby of metal detecting. I believe that he searched for the gold right up to his death."

Hank had finally succeeded in getting his cigar lit and was filling his corner of the dining room with a haze of blue smoke. Juanita got up and opened a window.

"Don't tell me the old buzzard succeeded in finding it?" said Hank in a clear attempt to warn me off any further revelations.

"No, Uncle Ricky didn't find the gold," I said. "It was Aunt Geraldine who found it."

I looked over at Nancy. She had turned another two shades ruddier. She could easily have played a vine-ripened tomato in one of those produce commercials where they anthropomorphize fruit.

Chapter Thirty-One

"What complicates matters considerably," I said, "is that the gold discovered by my aunt was unearthed on a portion of the Little Tombstone property which had been deeded over—without my aunt's knowledge—to a third party."

"What third party?" Juanita demanded. "And why?"

"I understand it was in repayment of a debt," I said. "This puts me in a tenuous position as heir to my aunt's fortune, both from a legal standpoint and an ethical one."

"What if the legal owner of the land has no intention of laying claim to Geraldine's find?" said Nancy, rising to her feet. "Perhaps, she—the legal owner, I mean—has amends to make with your aunt," Nancy said and sat down.

"That would remove one significant obstacle to my inheritance of my great aunt's estate," I said, "but it still begs the question of whether Geraldine would—had she known what I know now—have chosen to leave me everything, rather than leaving the bulk of her estate to her immediate family."

"I think I speak for us all when I say I'm a bit confused as to why you are telling us all this," Juanita said.

"I called you all here today to take advantage of the collective wisdom of the community," I said. "Every person here has been significantly affected in some way by the contents of my Great Aunt Geraldine's will, and I've called you here today to help me honor the wishes of Geraldine while taking into consideration that she might have made a different decision, had she known the whole truth."

"The whole truth about what?" Juanita persisted. "I'm sorry, Emma, but you are being very unclear."

Georgia spoke up from the back of the room.

"I think I can help explain. It has to do with my mother and sister."

"Georgia had nothing to do with Freida's death," I hastily interjected.

"But I did have something to do with getting written out of my grandmother's will. I'm sure at least a few of you were aware that Grams thought we were trying to get her declared incompetent so my mother could get power of attorney."

A few heads nodded, but there was an equal number of blank looks.

"I truly believed Grams was losing it, at first, anyway," Georgia continued. "When I found out it wasn't true, I found a way to put a stop to it."

I carried on where Georgia left off.

"Aunt Geraldine was so angry that she cut her daughter and both of her granddaughters out of the will," I said. "But she never knew that Georgia was innocent of wrongdoing, that's why I'm questioning the fairness of the will."

"I have a suggestion," Juanita said. "I think we can all agree that Geraldine left Little Tombstone to Emma because she believed that Emma would take care of it the best she could."

Everyone's heads were nodding except for Hank's, but since he didn't snort, I took that as a sign of agreement.

"My proposition is this," Juanita continued, "Half of Geraldine's estate be reserved for the preservation of Little Tombstone and that Emma consider gifting Georgia a quarter of the remaining money."

"Can I do that?" I turned to Mr. Wendell.

"There are considerable tax implications," he replied, "but it would be possible. I'd suggest setting up a non-profit foundation for the preservation of Little Tombstone and appointing a board of directors to oversee it."

"I'll do it," I said, "and I can't think of a group more qualified to be the board than those assembled here."

I meant it, too, although I had misgivings about Hank.

After that, events moved quickly. Georgia and I worked with Mr. Wendell to set up a trust to ensure the future of Little Tombstone, and then we set to work returning Little Tombstone to a state of reasonable repair.

I floated the idea of hiring Oliver as a full-time salaried employee if I could get a work permit for him, but he informed me that there was no need to apply for a permit. His mother was a US citizen living in Australia, and, in fact, Oliver himself had been born in San Francisco.

Georgia and her son settled into their new home. Georgia's son, Maxwell, who'd never had a pet other than a goldfish, was fascinated by Earp.

Earp was less than enthusiastic about being followed from room to room and forcibly having his belly scratched, but the pug put up with Maxwell's attentions because the kid was a messy eater. Georgia didn't belong to the no-snacks-between-meals school of parenting, so if Earp stayed in Maxwell's orbit, there was a very real chance of being caught in a hailstorm of crumbs.

Georgia gradually came to terms with her twin's demise. It was a complicated cycle of grief, anger, regret, and a pervasive sense of horror over the circumstances surrounding Freida's death.

It turned out that the day Marco went to the Santa Fe Sheriff's Office, he'd confessed both to the murder of Freida and to the acts of vandalism and sabotage that had briefly plagued Little Tombstone.

However, when Nancy confessed to her part in Freida's killing, Marco was no longer considered a suspect in Freida's death. He served a stint in Juvenile Detention for vandalism and arson. It was a hard lesson, but I was confident Marco would never again get involved with anyone offering him money to commit acts of vandalism.

Nearly six months to the day after Freida was shot, Nancy went to trial on charges of wrongful death. After a mere three hours of deliberation, she was found not guilty by a jury of her peers.

Nancy never did formally confess to her role in the disappearance of the Halversons, nor did my cousin Abigail, but, acting on an anonymous tip, the Santa Fe Police Department were able to match the DNA of Stacy Halverson's living niece to one set of remains dug up from underneath the trailer court of Little Tombstone. No living relatives were ever located for Greg Halverson, but nevertheless, the case was closed, and the mingled remains of the Halversons were given a final resting place in the old cemetery overlooking the village of Amatista.

Without naming names, I asked Mr. Wendell if anyone could still face charges in a case of hit-and-run from thirty years ago, but he told me that the statute of limitations had passed.

I decided to keep the details surrounding the Halversons' disappearance to myself. I also never told Hank the truth about the lights he'd seen behind Little Tombstone. I let him believe that Oliver and I had managed, single-handedly, to purge Amatista of an ongoing alien invasion.

I figured if I had any hope of turning Little Tombstone back into the thriving roadside attraction it once was, it couldn't hurt for the place's oldest resident to have complete confidence in my abilities to complete any task, no matter how daunting.

I kept my secrets but finally pried out Hank's. The reason Hank paid no rent was due to his role in assisting Aunt Geraldine in converting her antique gold pieces into cold hard cash. It seemed that Hank's lady friend Phyllis owned a pawnshop, and her gold buyer at the time was not the sort to ask questions.

On the day of Nancy's exoneration, Georgia and I went to visit Freida's grave. Maxwell insisted on coming along and bringing Earp with him.

I didn't think it was appropriate to bring a dog to a cemetery, but my protests were overruled. I was worried that Earp would try to mark his territory by lifting his leg on Freida's headstone, or that he'd decide to do his business on the stone slab that covered the grave, but he did neither of those things.

The pug seemed happy enough when I lifted him from his spot in the back seat beside Maxwell and set him on the ground. Earp sniffed excitedly at unfamiliar smells all the way to the section of the cemetery that contained my cousin's grave, but when we approached the stone marking Freida's final resting place, Earp bristled and backed away, growling.

Nothing could induce him to move any closer, so we left Earp where he'd planted himself in the dusty path, charging Maxwell to keep a firm grip on his leash while Georgia and I went closer to pay our respects.

Whoever said that dogs are a better judge of character than humans are spoke a wealth of wisdom.

The End

Want to help other readers like you find this little mystery? Reviews don't have to be long and complicated. Please take a minute or two to leave a brief review on the site where you purchased this book.

Want to be notified of Celia's promotions and new releases? Follow Celia on Amazon, BookBub, or signup for Celia's newsletter at **celiakinsey.com**

Sample First Chapter of Lonesome Glove

I don't know if you've ever tried to make tamales, but it's not as easy as it looks; at least it's not as easy as Juanita, my late grandmother's closest friend, and proprietress of the Bird Cage Café, makes it look. When Juanita makes tamales, she assembles eight at a time.

I stood in the kitchen of the Bird Cage and watched as Juanita slopped hot cooked masa on the middle of each boiled corn husk, smoothing it with the back of the spoon as she went. Then she added dollops of filling to the middles. Finally, in what took about 60 seconds, for her, she rolled all eight tamales into neat little corn husk bundles, ready to go into the steamer.

I'd been working on rolling and rerolling a single miserable overstuffed tamale in the same time Juanita had made sixteen.

In my pitiable version of the classic Mexican dish, the masa mixed with the filling and spilled out of the split husk to decorate the outside of the misshapen bundle.

I've never been good in the kitchen, and I had already repeatedly congratulated myself that I'd not dropped anything on the floor or down the front of the sturdy apron Juanita had insisted on tying me into.

I had a feeling that Juanita was regretting that she'd offered to teach me to make tamales. She'd tried to teach me to cook when I was a teenager. It had not been an outstanding success. I think Juanita assumed I'd make a better student now that I was past thirty. Sadly, untrue.

While I disassembled my misshapen abomination against Mexican cuisine in general and corn-based products in particular,

Chamomile, Juanita's head waitress at the Bird Cage, mentioned that there'd been a recent spate of mail thefts in the village of Amatista.

"Stealing the mail?" I asked as I took a spoon and tried to scrape my masa/green chili/chicken mixture back into the center of the husk. "Is somebody stealing mail in general or one person's mail in particular?"

"Roberta Haskell says the money her son's been sending her is getting stolen, but my mother has been keeping a lookout for the envelopes in her mailbag and hasn't seen anything from Roberta's son come through for months."

Chamomile's mother, Katie, is one of my tenants in the trailer court out behind the Bird Cage Café. She's also the village of Amatista's sole mail carrier. Katie delivers to the rural postal customers, which, if you subtract the 30-odd people who live in the village proper, is pretty much all of them.

I tried to place Roberta Haskell and failed, which didn't surprise me, seeing as I'd only been back in Amatista since early November, and it was only the second week in January.

Out in the dining room of the Bird Cage, I heard a small boy yell "Tiiimber," followed by a crash and the high-pitched barking of our pug-in-residence, Earp.

My cousin Georgia—second cousin, if I'm going to split hairs—had insisted that it was high time to take the Christmas decorations down from the dining room, much to her young son Maxwell's sorrow.

I suspected the crash had been the aluminum Christmas tree falling over, and doubtless, Maxwell and Earp had had something to do with the toppling of the tree.

"Does Mrs. Haskell get her mail delivered?" I asked Chamomile.

Everyone living in the village proper has to go pick up their mail from the bank of boxes in the tiny adobe post office on the edge of town. I couldn't imagine how anyone but a postal employee would manage to steal mail from the bank of little boxes inside the post office proper.

"Mrs. Haskell is on the rural route," said Chamomile. "Mom tells me she's still getting bills and an avalanche of junk mail. Just the money from her son is going missing."

"How long has this been going on?" I asked.

Chamomile didn't know.

"You go to church with Roberta, don't you?" I asked Juanita, who had been uncharacteristically quiet that morning.

"Last Sunday, at church, Roberta was telling me all about it," Juanita said. "I got the impression it has been a problem for several months."

When Juanita says "church," she's referring to the weekly Sunday meetings Freddy Fernandez, the devout barber, holds in the back of his barbershop next door to the Bird Cage Café.

"Is her son sending cash?" I asked. "Because if he's sending checks, wouldn't anybody else have trouble cashing them?"

Juanita said she didn't know and moved the conversation on to my own personal troubles. "Has Frank signed your divorce papers yet?"

I told Juanita that Frank had not.

Shortly before Christmas, my soon-to-be-ex-husband Frank had inexplicably and abruptly decided that he could not live without me—this despite having allowed his mistress/office manager Shirley to take the money I'd earned from finally selling a screenplay and blow it on the roulette tables in Vegas.

Frank remained entirely unrepentant about the whole sordid affair, yet vowed he was going to "win me back." I'd suggested that winning back lost property was more a matter he should be addressing with his ladylove Shirley.

"I was mistaken about Shirley," Frank had said. "She's nothing compared to you."

It was at that moment that I realized that Shirley, too, had left him. Frank never has been a man who copes well on his own. He can't even iron his own shirts.

"Frank will sign the papers eventually," I told Juanita. "He'll have to."

I had no intention of getting back together with Frank, an intention that my divorce lawyer, Mr. Wendell, had quietly affirmed. It was typical, Mr. Wendell told me, for the offending party in a divorce to have last-minute remorse over the consequences of their actions.

This discussion of my messy personal life was cut short by the entrance of Ledbetter.

Marcus Ledbetter parks his trailer on the second of the three occupied spots in the trailer court out back of the Bird Cage.

He's a bit of a recluse, which my Great Aunt Geraldine always insisted was due to coming back with PTSD after his tour of duty in Afghanistan.

My Aunt Geraldine and Ledbetter had been close in the years leading up to her death, so close that he'd taken my aunt Geraldine's nest egg and turned it into a small fortune. Ledbetter is something of a stock-picking genius, and nobody knows it but me.

Ledbetter certainly doesn't look like he's involved in high finance. He looks more like a member of one of your less-reputable fraternities of motorcycle enthusiasts, but he's a gentle and generous soul under all that black leather, scowl, and muscle.

Ledbetter shifted from one enormous booted foot to the other and turned his intense blue eyes on me.

"I'd like to add an item to the agenda."

Ledbetter was referring to the agenda for the meeting of the newly formed Little Tombstone Preservation board. Not long after I'd inherited Little Tombstone from my Great Aunt Geraldine, I'd decided to take the bulk of the considerable sum I'd inherited along with the ramshackle roadside tourist attraction and place it in trust to be used for the preservation of the crumbling monstrosity.

The newly formed Little Tombstone Preservation board consisted of the current tenants of Little Tombstone, Nancy Flynn, our neighbor and the mayor of Amatista, my cousin Georgia, and me. For various reasons, the first two meetings of the board had been far less productive than I'd hoped.

"What do you want us to discuss?" I asked Ledbetter.

"Parliamentary procedure."

I'd rather lost control of the last meeting. When I'd brought up the subject of repainting the row of buildings that fronted Main Street, two distinct camps had emerged. One was strongly in favor of brownish-yellow, and the opposing camp was equally set on a brownish-gray. A minority of one (Hank Edwards, proprietor of Little Tombstone's Curio Shop and the Museum of the Unexplained) made an impassioned case for grayish-green.

It had been a trying experience, with no conclusive outcome. I was toying with the idea of resigning my position as chairperson and letting someone with a great deal more natural authority take over the role, someone like Ledbetter.

"You won't reconsider taking over the role of chair?" I asked Ledbetter.

He gave me a barely perceptible nod and an unblinking stare.

"I will not," he said, "but I do have a few suggestions."

End of sample

Sample Chapter of Fit to be French Fried

This is a sample from the first short mystery in the *Felicia's Food Truck One Hour Mysteries Omnibus Edition.*

When Mrs. Dunn said she'd like to kill her pesky parrot, I had no inkling that it was Mrs. Dunn herself who'd be darkening death's door by sundown.

Mrs. Dunn was not my all-time favorite customer. Technically, she wasn't a customer at all in the sense that she never bought anything. Either Mrs. Dunn had lost her driver's license, or she liked to walk for her health, but almost every day she'd stop in on her way to or from the Whispering Palms Senior Living Complex. It didn't matter if she was walking to the supermarket, or to Senior Bingo at the Baptist Church, or to the Dollar Store; Mary Dunn never failed to take advantage of the ice water dispenser we keep next to the food truck.

Even Marge, who carries her belongings around in a black plastic bag and sleeps on the porch of the old house that serves as Bray Bay's tiny public library, occasionally springs for a small French fry on principle.

"Because I always drink your water," she'll say.

Mrs. Dunn was burdened by no such sense of obligation.

"Surely, you don't really mean it when you say you want to kill Polly?" I said.

Mrs. Dunn sipped ice water from the cup she held in her right hand and tightened her grip on her shopping trolley with her left, an arm firmly clamped across the bright blue handbag she wore slung across her body. Mrs. Dunn was the sort who believes thieves are always lurking just out of the corner of one's eye, intent on stealing one's low-fat yogurt, bran cereal, and multi-vitamins.

"I do mean it. I really hate that bird," Mrs. Dunn insisted. "The only reason that stupid parrot is still alive is that they've been after me for years to get rid of her. That dratted bird is driving me crazy, but I can't get rid of the blasted thing on principle."

"Perhaps your parrot is driving 'them' crazy, too?" I suggested. I didn't know who "they" were, and I wasn't about to ask. If I asked, Mrs. Dunn would remain for another ten minutes, airing her grievances and scaring away the paying customers.

"Well, Felicia," said Mrs. Dunn, "can't stand around all day chatting."

Rather than placing her used paper cup into the recycling bin, she set it down on a table I'd just wiped clean. I glanced over at the serving window of the food truck. My cook, Arnie, was scowling at the back of Mrs. Dunn's head. Arnie is a stickler for recycling.

Mrs. Dunn took an even firmer hold on her trolley, adjusted her bright blue handbag so it hung low across her belly—the better to keep an eye on it—and shuffled off down the street back toward Whispering Palms.

We get a lot of business from the residents of Whispering Palms despite the retirement complex having its own dining room. Whispering Palms' promotional leaflet proclaims they provide a gourmet menu approved by a state-licensed nutritionist, but most of the residents prefer my fare: good old-fashioned hot dogs, juicy hamburgers, and crispy French fries, golden brown, with a light dusting of salt.

I was just wiping up the water ring left behind by Mrs. Dunn's abandoned cup when we got another customer, a paying one this time.

Prue, who also lives at Whispering Palms, is sweet as pie, albeit a little loopy. Even Frank, Arnie's grumpy, geriatric Dachshund, likes her, although that may be mostly down to the dog biscuits Prue carries in her handbag.

At the sound of Prue's voice, Frank emerged from the shaded underside of the food truck and waddled over to lean expectantly against the old lady's ankles.

"Dear me," Prue said as she scratched behind Frank's ears with the tip of her cane and examined the menu written on the chalkboard propped against one of the tires. "Felicia, you must have added more options."

It's the same menu we've had for the past three years, but every time Prue sees it, she's convinced we've completely overhauled our selection.

"I think I feel like a hot dog," Prue said. "Or maybe a hamburger. Or grilled cheese. I see you do salads. Salads are healthier. Maybe I'll have a salad."

Prue reached into her handbag and took out a dog biscuit for Frank before stepping back and scrutinizing the menu board for another full minute.

"No, I don't feel like a salad," she said firmly. "Give me a large chili fry, Arnie, with plenty of cheese sauce."

"No can do," Arnie said. "I can give you anything on the menu except French fries. The vat is on the blink."

I'd like to say that this equipment failure is an isolated incident, but our fry vat goes out every other week. Arnie usually gets it working again in an hour or two. I keep insisting we should just buy a new one, but the truth is, I can barely pay Arnie **and** my rent, and Arnie knows it.

"I'm sorry, Prue," I said, "whatever you'd like, it's on the house."

I knew I'd get a lecture from Arnie. He insists the reason we struggle to make a profit is that I give away too much free food.

"You don't have to do that," Prue insisted, but she took a free hamburger.

"You'd better take off," I told Arnie, "or you won't make it to your niece's recital on time."

"Is it 3:30 already?" Arnie looked at his wrist, but he wasn't wearing a watch.

"Must be," I said. "The school bus just went by."

In another ten minutes, we'd get a smattering of after-school customers, but I could handle them alone, especially since the fryer was down for the count.

"Recital?" Prue asked.

"Sammy, my niece," Arnie said, trying not to look proud. "She's having her piano recital today, just down the street at the middle school."

"That's nice," Prue said as she bit into her hamburger. "Is this a new recipe? I've never had it before."

It's not a new recipe, and Prue's eaten our hamburgers at least a hundred times.

Arnie raised his eyebrows at me over the top of Prue's head and mouthed, "See you later," before he took off on foot toward the middle school.

I sat down at the table with Prue and started to speak, but my attention was diverted by an ambulance headed in the direction of Whispering Palms, lights on, siren silent.

"Oh, dear, oh dear," said Prue. "I wonder who it is this time."

The residents of Whispering Palms are always getting hauled off to the hospital. Most of them come back, but some of them end up in nursing homes, or worse yet, the cemetery.

"Is someone at Whispering Palms trying to make Mary Dunn get rid of her parrot?" I asked, half because I wanted to know, and half because I wanted to distract Prue from wondering which of her friends was headed to the hospital.

"You mean Polly? I guess Polly is a bit of a nuisance," Prue said, "but I live on the other side of the complex, so that bird doesn't bother me much."

"Whose feathers has Polly ruffled, then? Mrs. Dunn implied that someone was mounting a campaign to deprive her of her parrot."

"I bet it's that Irma McFee," said Prue. "I've never warmed to Mary Dunn, but that Irma is downright vicious."

Prue doesn't usually express strong opinions about people.

"What do you mean, 'vicious'?" I asked

I never got my answer, because two police cars, sirens blaring, rushed past. I expected the sirens to fade into the distance, but instead, they cut off abruptly.

"I think those patrol cars stopped just down the street," I told Prue. "I'm going to jog around the block and take a look."

"What if somebody comes?" Prue protested.

"If anybody comes, tell them I'll be right back," I told Prue. "And if any packs of middle schoolers show up, don't let them put their dirty little mitts in the pickle jar."

End of Sample

Made in United States
North Haven, CT
25 April 2022

18529853R00136